WHEN SUMMER FINDS US

A DIAMOND BEACH ROMANCE

RICHARD FREEBORN

SHORT STORY COLLECTIONS

- Mageweaver
- A Frailty of Heroes
- Call Me Rhys
- A Bag of Bodies
- The Beach Bar on the Dune
- Ceres to Vesta
- Where Infinity Begins

THE SERPENT TRILOGY

- The Head of the Serpent
- The Body of the Serpent
- The Tail of the Serpent

DIAMOND BEACH

- When Summer Finds Us
- When Winter Ends

For everyone who took a leap of faith and declared their love

WHEN SUMMER FINDS US

A DIAMOND BEACH ROMANCE

RICHARD FREEBORN

Sue used her legs and feet to push the wheeled executive chair away from the paper-strewn desk that had held her captive all afternoon. She pushed the bifocals up onto her forehead and kneaded her knuckles into her eyes in an attempt to wipe away the tired, gritty feeling in them.

She had spent all afternoon working on rows and columns of numbers for the hospital's budget next year. The hours in front of the computer screen left her with more than tired eyes. She had a dull headache and an uncomfortable, sour feeling in her stomach.

Sue knew the feeling wasn't just from the coffee she'd drunk to stay alert. She became a nurse to help and care for people. The further she climbed the ladder of achievement, the more she became a bureaucrat and the less she used her nursing skills.

The office that had once been her sanctuary now felt like a cage. A gilded cage, but still a cage.

Sue pushed to her feet, settled her glasses back on her

nose. The unsettled feeling in her stomach told her something was happening.

Something she needed to address.

The first time she experienced the feeling, she was a student nurse, and it saved the life of a patient. During the last thirty-plus years, the feeling had never failed her, even during the dark days immediately after Ben died.

Sue blinked the sudden tear away, then wiped her eye and settled her glasses back on her nose. It still surprised her how the sorrow, grief, and anger could return when she least expected it.

She took a long breath, patted her strawberry-blonde hair into place, and shrugged a white coat with her name stenciled over the left breast over her pale blue blouse.

She saved the spreadsheet and locked her computer. She'd had to issue a written warning about computer security just last week. It wouldn't look good if she was the next violation.

The hallway outside her office, with its neutral, soothing gray paint and tang of antiseptic and bleach cleaner was empty.

Sue checked her watch.

Just after six-thirty in the evening. Most of the administrative staff had left, and the offices along the hallway were dark. The outpatient entrance was closed. Anything happening would be in or around the Emergency Room.

She pushed through an access door out into the hallway leading to the Emergency Room.

The silence was replaced by a maelstrom of noise.

How had she missed this?

Why had no-one called her?

Sue made a mental note to talk to her staff, then focused her attention to what was happening in the Emergency Room lobby.

The sliding double doors at the front were closed, and

there were no ambulances in the drive-up. That was one blessing. Sue wasn't so sure about the group of men and women sitting in wheelchairs or crowded on the benches in the hallway. They looked like outpatients from the therapy unit and should have been taken home at least an hour ago.

In the waiting room by the reception desk, two boys, eleven or twelve years old, sat curled in their parents' embrace. One cradled his head in his hands; the other held an arm twisted to an awkward angle. Both youths wore base-ball uniforms.

After wondering why the boys still waited, Sue offered a double prayer of thanks that Emily, her only child, showed no interest in or aptitude for sport of any kind.

Sue felt her lips twitch up. It may not have been sports, but Emily had caused heartache in other ways.

And then she heard a voice.

Deep, frustrated, and insistent.

A person on the edge.

Sue moved quickly, her low heels clicking on the tile floor as she headed to the reception desk, aware that people were shifting their attention from the tall muscular man at the desk to her.

Lord, she so hated much attention, and forced herself to ignore it. This man was on the edge, and he needed to be calmed down before he became a security event.

She noted the jeans, the battered brown leather jacket, sleeves pushed up almost to his elbows, and unzipped to reveal a crisp white button-down. She saw how his big hands gripped the edge of the counter. The way the muscles in his upper body bunched as he leaned forward so his breath clouded the security screen.

"What do you mean you can't find my mother? The ambulance brought her here over four hours ago, and you lost her?"

His voice was low, commanding, expecting obedience. There was a familiarity in the tone Sue couldn't place.

She closed her eyes for a moment, wishing she was back in her office. If she did that, then why did she complain so much about not helping patients?

And where was security?

She gauged the reach of his arms and hands if he turned violent, positioned herself so she could back away, and said.

"It's been a busy day. If you give me your mother's name, and yours, I can help. I'm the Director of Nursing."

He swung around when he heard her voice. His hands came off the counter. He ran a hand through the gray stubble on his scalp. His ice-blue eyes fixed her with his focus.

The gesture with his hair, such as it was. The eyes. The way his head tilted to the left as he looked at her.

Sue's memory flashed back nearly forty years.

The last year at Diamond Beach High School.

Long before she met Ben at Johns Hopkins.

He was someone whose name came up occasionally when she reminisced with the small circle of friends she'd kept since High School.

Someone she never expected to see again.

"Richard Miller, isn't it," she said, deliberately not offering her hand. "Give me a moment and we'll find your mother."

The look on his face shifted from anger, and frustration to an expression that looked stunned.

She wasn't sure what to make of that. Instead, she pressed her advantage.

"You need to move out of the way." She gestured at the couple behind him, and the baseball brothers.

"There are other people looking for information and help."

He frowned, turned his head to take in the line, then bent to the elderly couple immediately behind him.

"I'm sorry," he said.

"It's good you worry about your mother," the woman said. "I'm sure she's here, and I know Sue will find her for you."

He turned away from the couple, and looked at her. Really looked at her.

"Susie Terrell?"

Lord. After all these years. It really was him.

"Most people call me Sue now, Richard. Or Susan. Susan Williams."

Some of the tension left his body as he took a step away from the counter, giving the woman and her husband space to step forward and talk to the receptionist.

He gave her a smile, and it brightened his face, lifting away some of the anger and tension.

"Pretty much everyone except Mama calls me Rick these days. Are you sure you can find Mama?"

Sue looked at the way he stood, the way his gray hair was cropped to stubble, a ragged scar on his forearm that snaked up under the sleeves of the rolled-back white button-down where it poked out from the sleeves of the leather jacket.

There was something in his blue eyes. Hurt, pain, and something she couldn't identify.

He was very different from the gangly, uncoordinated teenager who'd declared his love under the bleachers at the end of their senior year.

A passion she hadn't felt, and couldn't return.

Sue knew her rejection that night had hurt him. She had spent hours wondering how she could have handled it better, then heard Richard, Rick, had left Diamond Beach. There were many rumors about what had happened to him.

Looking at him now, Sue guessed that the one about volunteering for the Army was most likely the true one.

"Diamond Beach Medical Center isn't that big," Sue said.

"If we can't find her here, we'll call the ambulance service and work out where she was taken."

Sue considered taking him back to her office, then caught herself. That violated just about every safety rule in the hospital, and the advice she gave every nurse, doctor, and administrator.

"Let me check on one of the spare monitors," she said. "I can't let you behind the counter, but I'll talk you through everything I'm doing."

"I get it," he said, and she knew he understood.

Sue waved her access card at the panel, waited for the beep and green light, then pushed inside. She logged into the computer, typed in the family name, and paused, trying to remember his mother's name.

She looked up through the plastic security panel to ask him.

Rick stood to one side, his right side close to the counter, his hands behind his back in the parade rest stance she'd watched in public broadcast documentaries.

He wasn't at rest. She could see it in his shoulders and the way his head moved in slow arcs as he watched the reception area.

Definitely Rick, and not Richard.

Sue tapped gently on the plastic panel, waited until his attention shifted and his blue eyes focused on her.

"What's her first name?"

"Frances."

Now she remembered. It was a tradition in his family that the eldest child was named Frank. Rick's grandparents made the mistake of having a girl as their first child, and it caused a split in the family. Sue had never understood the reasons. She wasn't sure Rick knew them, but it had brought the family to Diamond Beach.

Frances Miller.

Nothing.

She let her fingers rest on the keyboard, glanced up. Rick was back to watching the room. She didn't think he was really seeing any of it.

She tried variations of both names, even trying Francis instead of Frances.

Still nothing.

Sue leaned back in the chair, called across to the receptionist.

"Tracie, did we have an emergency come in today? One that went straight to OR or ICU?"

The woman looked over, scratched her pert nose, then pushed a hand through her auburn hair. She considered the question for a moment, then nodded.

"It was an elderly woman. She coded as they brought her out of the ambulance. We've been swamped what with outpatient transport being such a mess and I never had time to enter the details."

Sue took a long breath, swallowed the angry retort that came to her, and said.

"Next time, call me."

She reached for the phone on the console and stabbed at the numbers with her forefinger.

Sue was grateful Rick remained turned away as she spoke to Sarah, the senior ICU nurse.

She replaced the receiver and took another long breath. This was the part of the job she liked the least. Especially when she knew the family.

Diamond Beach wasn't that big. Not for the locals.

Rick's head turned toward her as she came through the door. Sue moved close to him so the conversation was private, then wished she hadn't.

The warmth of his body enveloped her, and deep down,

those lady parts, which had been quiet since Ben got ill, stirred and threatened to wake up.

She pushed the emotions away from the front of her head, put on the detached, professional persona that had gotten her through so many similar situations in the past.

"Your mom called her alert system with chest pains earlier today. She had a heart attack as the ambulance arrived, and she's in the ICU at the moment. She's stable, and the doctors want to examine her tomorrow morning."

"Surgery?"

Sue shrugged. "Possibly. I don't want to second-guess the cardiologist."

TWO

Second guess.

Rick felt every decision he'd made in the last year had been a second guess, or third guess.

He pushed the thought away. The consequences of those decisions were out of his hands now.

For the first time since he'd come through the doors searching for his mother, Rick looked around and really looked at the waiting area.

The air was heavy with the sharp aroma of antiseptic, stale coffee, and that peculiar institutional boiled cabbage smell he always associated with hospitals, barracks, and government hallways.

The reception desk was behind him. The entry doors in front were closed at the moment, the ambulance parking bay empty. Inside the doors, four rows of blue plastic chairs offered places to sit. From the pained looks on the few occupants, the hard plastic was as uncomfortable as it looked.

Eight wheelchairs were clustered behind the chairs and near the cream-painted back wall. Each wheelchair had an occupant with similar cropped haircuts, shirts and shorts. He spotted missing arms and legs among the group, and a man with bandages across his eyes.

Rick felt a shiver of fear ripple down his back. Every time he saw an injury like that, he prayed he'd never become blind. He'd take losing an arm or a leg, even accept a disfiguring injury to his head and body.

The prospect of being left blind scared him more than most anything else.

Rick guessed from the way they sat, and the way they huddled together so their conversations were private, that they were veterans.

The indistinct murmur of the veteran's conversation mixed with the noise from the big-screen television. Rick glanced at the flickering images, grateful it was a cooking show and not the news.

He didn't think he could take the news channels at the moment.

To his left, beyond the reception desk, the automatic double doors were closed, a heavy tint on the glass preventing a view of the triage rooms beyond.

Rick shook his head. A month ago, walking into a building without checking the environment would likely have got him killed.

He turned back, and for the first time, studied his companion.

Sue was taller than he remembered, and fuller in the waist. Her hair was shorter. It no longer cascaded down her back in a blonde waterfall. Now her hair was strawberry blonde and curled gently over the collar of her white coat. Streaks of silver threaded through the blonde, giving her a regal look.

She wore a powder blue blouse under the coat, gray slacks, and sensible flat shoes. He wondered if the legs inside the slacks were as long, firm, and shapely as he remembered from that summer.

She was still the most beautiful person he'd ever met, and absolutely the last person he expected to encounter in Diamond Beach.

He kept his left hand behind his back and flexed the fingers one by one. Little finger first, then through the rotation to his forefinger and thumb. It was a grounding technique he'd learned at Quantico all those years ago when he still lacked confidence.

A way of calming himself without making it obvious.

And here he was, back in Diamond Beach, and as tongue-tied with Susie, Sue, as he'd always been.

"Can I see Mama?"

Sue gave him a look he couldn't interpret. The look was just like the unspoken assessment from an experienced NCO when first introduced to a new lieutenant still wet behind the ears.

For a moment, Rick thought she was going to say no, tell him he had to return during visiting hours.

"I'll take you up there," she said.

There was compassion and sympathy in her emerald eyes, and that look took him back to the bleachers at Diamond Beach High all those years ago.

It had been a hot and humid Friday evening in July, a week after graduation. Dry lightning flickered blue and silver out in the Gulf. There was a promise of rain, and the bugs chittered in the darkness.

They weren't even dating or drinking, although some others had acquired a case of beer and were working through it with enthusiasm.

He'd been an idiot to say anything.

Something had compelled him to tell Sue how he felt,

even though she'd never shown she thought of him as anything more than one of their group of friends.

It had been the ultimate piece in the jigsaw puzzle of decisions that sent him to the Marine Corps.

"ICU is on the fourth floor. We'll take the stairs if you're up for it," she said.

Rick looked at her. Nodded.

He wondered if it was a challenge or genuine concern that he might not be able to climb the four flights. Yes, he was exhausted, but he didn't think he looked that bad. Rick ran a hand through the stubble of hair on his head and turned to follow Sue when a voice called out.

"Colonel Rick? Colonel, is that you, sir?"

THREE

Sue heard the deep gravelly voice call Rick's name.

Colonel?

She felt Rick's hand on her arm, turned to look at him, and saw the concern on his face.

"Give me a moment," he said.

Sue nodded. When he released her, she felt the loss. Felt the heat on her forearm through the coat and blouse. She shook her head. Stupid. She hadn't seen the man in however many years, hadn't had a reaction like this since she and Ben were newly married.

Sue shook her head again. She didn't have time for teenage fantasies. She had a hospital to run.

And hasn't that been fun these last few years, a cynical voice whispered in her head.

Sue pushed the thought away and watched as Rick approached the man who had called out. He went down on his haunches, bringing his face level with the man in the wheelchair.

Both legs stopped at his knees. Above the waist he was a bull of a man, with wide shoulders and arms like the hams they used to hang in the butcher's shop. His hair was cropped to the same stubbly length as Rick's; his face lifted with surprise and pleasure as Rick clasped his hand.

She heard Rick say.

"Gunny Denson. I didn't know you were a Diamond Beach man. How are you holding up?"

The man's craggy face broke into a smile, pleased that Rick remembered his name.

"Staying with my sister, and better than I was, sir. I caught the wrong end of an IED in Be'er Sheva. I wish I'd been with you in Hebron."

"No. You don't."

There was a harsh, brutal edge to Rick's voice that sent a shiver through Sue's body.

When Rick spoke again, his voice was softer, but she could still hear the pain.

"It was Hebron when they first used the biologicals. We lost a lot of good Marines that week. Some who survived maybe shouldn't have."

The words shocked Sue. They went against everything she had worked for and believed in. She was about to speak when Denson said in a low voice she barely heard.

"Copy that, Sir. Had those same thoughts myself more than once."

There was understanding in Denson's voice. His tone brought back to Sue the half-heard conversations between the veterans. A comment. A nod. A shake of the head.

Over the years, Sue had worked around trauma but never experienced it first-hand like these men and women.

Sue made a mental note to talk with the staff serving the veterans as Rick reached into the side pocket of his leather jacket, pulled out a wallet and some cards. He peeled off a card and handed it to the other man.

"Call me if you get those thoughts again, Gunny. No

matter the time. That's an order. Now tell me what you're doing here at this hour?"

"Waiting for a ride. They've got some issues with transport again."

Rick reached down, gripped the man's shoulder.

"I have to go with Director Williams. If you're still here when I'm done, I'll take you myself."

Denson's brown eyes sparkled, and his voice was lighter, tinted with humor. "Don't know I have that much time left, sir. You officers always win the prettiest ladies."

"I lost this lady a long time ago," Rick said in a tone she couldn't interpret.

When he stood and turned back to her, there was something in his eyes.

Regret? Fear? Longing?

Maybe a combination of all three.

Sue wanted to ask him about the look. About Hebron She pushed the thought away. There were too many people around them. Too many people who'd gossip.

She'd only met him again ten minutes ago. It was too soon for those questions. Perhaps there would never be a right time, and perhaps, she admitted to herself; she wasn't prepared for the conversation.

Why have the conversation anyway?

Most likely when his mother recovered and returned to her home, he'd be gone again for another thirty or more years.

"We still good for the stairs?" he asked.

She nodded, not quite sure she could trust her voice at the moment.

They crossed to the secured door that led to the stairwell. Once again, Sue touched her badge to the reader, waited for the beep and the green light.

Rick pulled the door open as she said.

"Why did you join the Army? Sorry, the Marine Corps?"

"I couldn't afford the flight to France."

He held the access door open so she could step through.

"Why France?" Sue asked as the door closed behind them with a hollow boom and a click as the security lock engaged.

"My plan was to go to the French Foreign Legion recruiting center in Paris, and then Aubagne for training."

Sue missed the next step. As her balance tipped, she felt a firm hand under her elbow, steadying and balancing her.

She felt a spark of something at Rick's touch. Another something stirred deep within her core.

"Getting clumsy," Sue said, forcing herself to ignore the sensation as they reached the first landing and continued up.

It was hard.

After a period of silence, and another flight of stairs, she returned to the original conversation. "You didn't speak French. None of us did."

"Still don't," he said. "The Legion teaches you."

"And this was because of what I said to you that night?"

Maybe they were going to have that conversation after all. She felt a shiver of horror that her words had been the trigger that set him on a different path in life.

"Not at all."

His tone was emphatic, allowing no argument. Sue paused before taking the next step, put a hand on the stair railing to balance herself and looked over at him. There was nothing in his expression that conflicted with his words.

"Then why?"

He responded with a deep, rumbling chuckle. Sue didn't want to think too hard about the way the sound resonated around the stairwell and inside her body. She gripped the stair rail a little harder and began climbing again as she listened to his answer.

"There was a lot of naive teenage romanticism involved," Rick said.

"That lasted maybe two days at Parris Island. I was certain I didn't want to follow my uncles into accounting, much as Mama wanted me to. I had no idea what I wanted to do with my life, but whatever it was, it wasn't behind a desk. The afternoons and weekends sailing our Beneteau convinced me of that."

He paused, and she remembered how he'd always been an outdoors hands-on person.

"The Corps tried to steer me the same way as the uncles, or into something legal with the Judge Advocate General," he continued. "An opportunity came up, and I applied to Special Operations Command. The overall attrition rate through selection and training is about sixty percent. I found I was good and loved it, still do, mostly. One of my officers saw something more in me and encouraged me to apply to Quantico."

"That's Officer Training, isn't it?" Sue knew that much from the outpatient veterans she spoke to.

"It is," he said, and gestured to the next landing with a two foot high number four stenciled on the wall in blue paint.

"Is this us?"

Sue nodded rather than speak and sound out of breath again. She believed she was in reasonable shape, but her breath was coming in long intakes. Her heart thudded hard against her chest, and her legs felt like rubber.

And Rick, damn him. Rick barely looked to be breathing heavily.

Sue swiped her card over the security panel, waited for the beep and green light, then pulled the door open.

FOUR

Rick put his hand on Sue's shoulder as she pulled the door open. He eased past her and checked the hallway.

To the left were doors on each side of the hallway, and an emergency exit at the end, the lettering in a vivid red. To the right, Rick saw more doors, the elevators and a nurses' station. A male nurse leaned on the counter, cradling a mug of coffee and talking with another nurse sitting behind the counter.

Sue shrugged his hand off her shoulder and pushed past him.

"This is a hospital. It's safe," she said as she walked toward the nurses' station.

"We were told Hadassah Hospital was safe," Rick said in a voice low enough that she wouldn't hear as he followed her along the hallway.

Something changed in her body, in the way her posture shifted. Her back straightened, shoulders pushed back, head up and swiveling from side-to-side, noting and remembering everything.

It was the same as when she'd first spoken to him in the reception area. A crisp edge of command, the expectation you'd do as she wanted.

A professional secure in her own environment.

He stood to one side as Sue spoke with the nurses, answered some questions, then thanked them.

"Room four-oh-six," Sue said, leading him past the elevators, then to a closed door on the right side of the hallway. She stopped with her hand on the door handle. She looked him directly in the eye, then her voice quiet, factual, devoid of emotion.

"The heart attack was a bad one. She's sedated and on blood thinners. Tomorrow, assuming she's stable enough, her medical team will do scans and more tests. After that, they'll determine the most appropriate treatment, which will probably include surgery."

"Is she going to pull through?"

Something flickered in Sue's green eyes.

Rick felt himself tense to prepare for the news. Or the lie. The assurances it was too soon to tell, and they were doing all they could for her.

Platitudes he'd heard too many times.

"Given the results I saw, her age, and what I know from experience, I'd say she has a fifty-fifty chance. And I shouldn't be telling you even that much."

"I know, and I appreciate the honesty," Rick said. Her openness surprised him.

Rick put his hand over Sue's on the door handle. He tried to ignore the spark of awareness that flowed between them at the touch. Tried to ignore her soft gasp and the soft intake of breath that drilled straight into his core. He pushed the door handle down.

Rick didn't want to release the door handle. Or Sue's

hand, but they couldn't stand in the open doorway like this for long.

It could get very awkward very quickly.

Rick let the door close behind them. The smell of antiseptic and strong disinfectant seemed to get stronger, making him breathe more shallowly. There were two beds in the room. The one farthest from the door was empty and stripped down to the mattress cover, the monitoring equipment disconnected and dark.

Frances, his mother, lay in the nearest bed.

Rick had visited a lot of hospitals. He had sat beside the bed of injured men and women, and much as the injuries suffered by his soldiers pained and disturbed him, seeing his mother like this was a painful thrust hard and deep into his gut.

She looked frail and sunken; her face looked like aged ivory against the crisp white sheets and the pillow that curled up around both sides of her head. Her once rich-brown hair had thinned, streaked now with gray and silver. An oxygen line was hooked under her nostrils and snaked away behind her ears. The machine on the wall above and beside the bed beeped a soft tune. The green lines of the heart and blood monitors traced a pattern across the screens. Inch-high red numbers flickered with pulse, heart rate, and blood oxygen levels.

Rick tore his gaze away from the monitor and focused again on his mother.

In the half-light he had to focus closely to make sure his mother still breathed. Her chest lifted and fell slowly, the monitoring machine the only sign she still lived.

"When did you last see her?"

Sue's voice was little more than a whisper. It came to him across the darkened room. Rick heard the shift in her tone, sensed the change in her posture from the way she'd spoken just now outside the room.

The professional was still there, but this was a question from a friend.

"A year ago. Maybe less. It was before we deployed to the Middle East. I didn't tell her where we were going, but I think she guessed."

"Hard not to. It was all over the news. The veterans around the hospital talked about nothing else."

Frances stirred then. Rick suspected their low voices had reached her subconscious. She shifted in the bed. Rick reached forward, took her right hand in his.

Her hand was cold, the skin dry like old paper ready to flake and crumble away. He felt the brittle bones beneath the skin with barely any muscle or sinew left to protect them. He was afraid to squeeze too hard in case he broke a bone in her hand.

"Mama. It's Richard. How are you feeling?"

Frances opened her eyes slowly, the blue in her irises faded and watery. She looked down at Rick's fingers curled round her right hand, glanced over at Sue.

She smiled then.

Rick saw the creases and lines smooth out from her forehead, felt the increased pressure of her grip on his hand, as she said.

"I'm so glad you two finally got together."

FIVE

"Mama."

There was a plaintive sound to Rick's voice as Frances slipped away back into sleep.

Sue stepped forward. It was an instinctive reaction. She felt a lurch in her stomach as she reached the opposite side of the bed, and picked up Frances' left wrist. She felt carefully along the bones in the older woman's arm searching for a pulse, and prayed she'd find one.

The beat was weak, but steady and consistent.

Sue looked up at the monitors that told her the same.

Only then did she have the courage to take a breath and shift her attention to Rick.

He looked stunned.

Carefully, he placed his mother's hand back on the cover, and slowly, reluctantly turned his head to look at her.

"She never knew," he said, his voice barely above a whisper.

"I never told her. I only ever told you."

Sue remembered her daughter Emily during her teen years. How she'd seen the way Emily looked at certain boys.

How their names came up more frequently in everyday conversation. The unexplained tears when that certain boy was dating someone else. Even worse, when that same boy dated one of Emily's friends.

"Mothers have special powers," she said, keeping her voice light.

"That sounds like the voice of experience."

Was that amusement in his voice?

"Most likely. My daughter Emily gave me some sleepless nights over the years."

She smiled at the memory. "My mom said it was payback for all the sleepless nights I caused her."

"It doesn't matter how old we are; parents still have a way of putting us in our place," Rick said.

This time the smile was on his face and in his voice.

Sue smiled back.

She felt something shift inside. She wasn't sure what it was. Perhaps a realization that no-one had smiled at her like that since before Ben was ill. Perhaps the realization that much as she had loved her job at first, now she was going through the motions. Perhaps a realization there was an opportunity to open a new chapter in her life.

It scared and excited her at the same time.

She took a deep breath and broke every rule in her book.

"I have a real coffee machine in my office, if you'd like some. It's better than you'll get from the machine."

Disappointment and regret clouded his face.

"I would, but I promised Denson a ride home."

Sue jerked her head, led him out of the room and toward the nurses' station.

She called down to Tracie, and didn't try to stop the relief and excitement that bubbled inside her when she learned the transport had arrived and departed.

"Your Sergeant Denson found his ride. We'll take the

elevator," she said, not giving him a chance to change his mind.

In the office, Sue busied herself with the coffee machine, letting the richness of the brew tease her nostrils.

Rick had looked around the room, like he was assessing ways in and out. Now, he stood by the window, phone to his ear, seemingly oblivious to his reflection in the tinted glass. She heard the phone at the far end ring and ring, then click over to voicemail.

Rick ended the connection without leaving a message. He turned away from the window, frustration twisted his face into a dark scowl. His blue eyes focused on something Sue couldn't see.

She had a feeling it was something that wasn't within a thousand miles of Diamond Beach.

"Is everything okay?" she asked.

He blinked, like she'd pulled him back from that distant place. The frustration on his forehead, around his mouth, and in his eyes smoothed away.

Rick smiled, but his tone was serious.

"I was trying to get an update on what's happening in Washington. Alex, my Executive Officer, isn't answering."

"Is that a bad sign?"

"I'm choosing to take it as a good sign," he said.

"Can you talk about it?"

His hesitation was obvious, then he shook his head. "Not really. Even talking with Alex is probably some sort of violation."

Sue wanted to ask if he was in trouble but knew he wouldn't give her a straight answer. For some reason that hurt, and she wasn't sure why. She'd met him for the first time in over thirty years barely two hours ago, and their last conversation all that time ago under the high school bleachers hadn't ended well

The final rumbling, hissing and gurgling of the coffee machine broke into her thoughts and she was glad for the distraction.

Rick held the mug close to his face so he could capture the aroma. Sue thought he looked cautious and careful, almost suspicious of the coffee.

"It is safe to drink," she said.

That brought a smile to his face, and life back into his eyes. He took a careful sip, then nodded appreciatively.

"Safe, and very good. For a part of the world that prides itself on its coffee, I've spent the last year drinking some really bad brews. Some of which I'm not even sure were coffee, and I don't mean the current enthusiasm for mushroom coffees."

"Mushrooms are not real coffee."

The words came out harsher, louder, and stronger than a Sue intended.

Rick's eyebrows lifted and his eyes twinkled. "Noted that Sue does not approve of mushroom coffee."

"I didn't say that," but she was laughing now, and had to admit he'd called it right. Mushrooms as coffee didn't seem right.

The earlier awkwardness was gone. Sue talked about nursing, and Emily. Rick told her stories about being a Marine, although she noted there were few specifics that would let her locate a time or a place. And he talked about Alex, his Executive Officer.

Alex was his protege, Sue guessed. Someone whose potential he'd nurtured and helped to grow. She'd done the same herself over the years, seen the potential in a nurse and helped that person grow into their ability. She was still in touch with some of them.

Sue realized the last inch or so of coffee in her mug was cold.

She really didn't want this time to end and was about to offer Rick more coffee when his phone rang.

He glanced at the screen and his face changed, the relaxed look from their conversation replaced with something closed and hard.

"I'm sorry," he said. "I need to take this."

"Alex?"

He nodded. "Yes. Thank you for the coffee, Sue. It was really good to reconnect with you. I hope I'll see you again."

"So do I," she said, but the office was empty. She heard the rumble of his voice out in the hallway, and wished he'd been able to stay longer.

It was still dark when Rick woke the next morning in the room he'd slept in as a teenager. His watch said it was just after five. He tossed, turned, and twisted on the lumpy mattress for a while, convinced it was the same mattress he'd had as a teenager before going to Parris Island.

Rick gave it up after forty minutes, shrugged into cargo shorts and a Marine Raider golf shirt, then padded across the house. He flipped on the kitchen light, started the coffee machine and looked around.

It felt strange to be in the house this early and not have his mother bustling around, wiping down the same counters she'd polished to a shine before going to bed the previous night.

As the coffee maker gurgled and threw the aroma of coffee into the air, Rick studied the family room beyond the kitchen. He saw his reflection on the eighty-inch flat-screen television on the opposite wall and thought he looked like how he felt.

A stranger.

Was that how Sue saw him? He wished he'd been able to stay and talk more with her. It was the first time in months he'd had a proper conversation with someone that didn't revolve around Israel or the decisions he'd made.

The return call from Alex hadn't told him much. The Inquiry Board had finished interviewing witnesses and retired to consider their findings. That could take days, weeks, months even.

He dragged his mind away from something he had no control over and forced himself to look away from the reflection.

The wall to the right of the television had the painting of the hotel where his parents were married. Underneath the painting was a wicker-framed loveseat. The red cushions faded to dark pink, looking as uncomfortable as his mattress. The polish on the arms of the loveseat was scuffed, scratched, and worn.

Opposite the painting, the French doors opened onto a small patio. Beside the door was his mother's recliner. There was a picture of his father on the table beside the recliner.

Rick hadn't looked at the photograph, really looked at it, in a very long time. The picture had been taken about a year before his father became ill. Rick realized with surprise, that he was now older than his father was in the picture.

It was something Rick had never thought about before. He wasn't sure he wanted to think about it now. His relationship with his father had been complicated. Where his father was mostly happy with indoor pursuits like chess or Go, Rick had always favored the outdoors, and it seemed the only thing they had in common was their love of sailing.

He shook his head as he reached into the cabinet for a mug. Some of it must have passed down because he'd excelled in strategy during his time at the war college.

Rick pushed the thoughts away for another time and poured the coffee.

The coffee smelled stale, like some of the field brews you could almost chew. Nothing like the smooth, rich, nutty espresso Sue had brewed last night.

The thought of Sue helped ease away the memories of his father.

She was the last person he expected to see in Diamond Beach. He hadn't expected to establish a connection with her, let alone feel the desire to see her again.

He stopped with the mug an inch from his mouth.

Where had that come from?

The thought came with the acceptance that he'd probably never fully gotten her out of his system. He smiled to himself at the revelation. Most likely, it explained why he'd never married, and why all the previous women in his life had challenged his commitment, called him a player, or demanded to know if there was someone else.

Rick thought about it as he sifted through the mail, barely registering the logos, return addresses, and postmarks.

He let his mind replay the memory of the way her blonde hair curved over her ear and floated over her neck. Smooth, he recalled, and no spots, wrinkles or lines like so many of his contemporaries.

He took a sip of the coffee and grimaced. Definitely field brew quality, he thought as he tried to concentrate on the mail. Real estate flyers, Medicare announcements and marketing, and a small pile of bills. Rick frowned at the logo on one letter.

Diamond Beach Marina.

It was probably another advertising flyer.

As he slit the envelope open with his thumb, there was a hammering on the front door.

The front door was on the left side of the living room. A result of many remodels and renovations over the years since the house was built in the 1950s. The glass in the front door was heavily frosted, but in the early morning light, Rick made out enough of the fuzzy, indistinct shape to know he was opening the door to a police officer.

The officer stepped back as Rick swung the door open.

Rick kept his hands in sight and was relieved the officer and his partner didn't have their weapons drawn.

Rick watched the partner take a step back and to the side in a move that covered his superior and gave him a clear field of fire at Rick if necessary.

A man who knew what he was doing.

Rick approved.

"Can I help you?"

The lead officer, Carter from the name tag, kept a serious expression on his long angular face. He looked to be about fifteen years younger than Rick, his partner much the same age. Carter's voice was deep, low, and rich with the accent of the panhandle.

"We had reports of an intruder at the house. Does Ms. Miller know you're staying here?"

"Probably not," Rick said. "She was asleep when I saw her at the hospital last night. I'm her son. My ID is in the bedroom. You're welcome to come with me."

Some of the tension in Carter's body eased away, but Rick could see he remained alert in case something changed.

Deliberately, Rick turned his back on the man. He gestured to the archway on his left that led off the living room to the guest bedrooms. He turned left, then left again, into his old bedroom.

Rick snagged his black leather wallet off the nightstand. He opened the wallet, then changed his mind. He closed the wallet and offered it to Carter.

"License and ID are inside."

Carter took the wallet, folded his fingers around the leather, then backed out into the living room.

Rick followed as Carter unfolded the wallet, slipped out the driver's license and the Department of Defense ID card. He studied both, then placed them on top of the leather and offered them back to Rick.

"Thank you, Colonel. You understand we have to check."

"I'm pleased you did," Rick said. He slotted the cards back in place and pushed the wallet into the back pocket of his shorts.

"Can I offer you coffee?"

For a moment, Rick thought Carter would accept, then the police officer shook his head. "Maybe another time. I hope your mother recovers. She's a lovely lady."

"One of the best," Rick said. He watched the two men walk down the paved walkway, closed the door and went back to his coffee.

The drink was cold.

He tossed the liquid into the sink and poured a fresh cup.

It didn't taste any better.

Rick grimaced and picked up the marina envelope, eased out the contents and couldn't hold back a murmur of surprise.

She'd kept the boat.

He shook his head and took another sip of the coffee. It was an automatic reaction.

It didn't taste as bad this time.

His father bought the forty-foot Beneteau secondhand, learned to sail, then taught his wife and Rick. They were some of the best times Rick remembered with his father. He wondered what shape the boat was in. It must be forty or fifty years old now, probably crusted with barnacles and slowly rotting at the dock.

He doubted the hospital would let him in to see his mother this early, so maybe a trip to the marina and see the state of the Beneteau.

The thrill of anticipation surprised him.

Sue slept badly. She tossed and turned most of the night, her mind on the conversation with Rick.

When the first flush of dawn lightened the sky, she rolled out of bed and into the shower. As the hot water cascaded over her, Sue was grateful today was Saturday. She knew she'd hit a sinker somewhere around mid-afternoon, and could drop onto the couch in the family room and doze for an hour or two with some mindless travel show as background.

Out of the shower and dried off, Sue slipped into an old pair of blue jeans and a Diamond Beach sweatshirt with frayed sleeves and a hole in the shoulder. She felt better when she reached the kitchen and smelled the rich chocolate aroma of the special-brand Ethiopian coffee as she measured spoonfuls into the machine. When the machine was running, she emptied the dishwasher; two mugs, three plates, and a handful of cutlery.

Sue set one mug on the counter beside the coffee machine and leaned back against the granite-topped island until the machine gurgled, spat, and hissed, then beeped it was complete.

The coffee tasted as good as it smelled. Sue let the hot liquid sit on her tongue for a moment and savored the flavor. Maybe a second cup would get her through the day. It wasn't like she had nothing to do. There were sheets to launder, floors to clean, and it had been at least ten days since she'd really cleaned the house.

If she lost herself in the cleaning, maybe she'd stop thinking about Rick.

The sudden chime of the bell at the front door brought her out of her reverie. She frowned, glanced at the clock on the wall beside the six-burner gas range.

Seven-thirty.

Sue checked her caller through the peephole, unhooked the security chain and opened the door.

She stepped back when Beth, her best friend since forever, pushed through before the door was fully open.

Where Sue had kept most of her slim figure over the years, Beth had, in her own words, gotten chunky.

"You have some 'splain' to do, Lucy," Beth said. She made her way to the kitchen and dropped the box she carried on the counter.

The aroma of fresh donuts drifted up from the box, meshed with the aroma of coffee.

Sue closed her eyes, gave a little groan of protest. Her stomach betrayed her and grumbled long and loud.

Beth's gray eyes sparkled triumphantly. The lid of the long box had a curly script that said the contents came from Laura's Donuts. Not true donuts. More like a croissant in a donut shape with toppings of blueberry, chocolate, or maple syrup and bacon, or apple and cinnamon.

Beth made a show of lifting the lid, and Sue saw her favorites. Chocolate and apple cinnamon.

Sue reached for the chocolate-covered donut. Beth moved the box away.

"First you give me the story, then I give you the reward."

"What story?"

Beth laughed. It was a musical tinkle that bounced around the kitchen, off the cabinets, the steel range hood, and the marble backsplash.

"You were seen avoiding the elevators and taking a big hunk of a man into the stairwell by the Emergency Room. So, pour me coffee and spill."

Sue wanted to go back upstairs, curl back up in bed, and resurface in six months or more.

She ran a hand through her hair.

Six months might not be long enough to quiet the story in Diamond Beach.

She squeezed past Beth, giving the back of her friend's head a glare. Sue reached into the cabinet, picked out a mug, and poured a second helping from the pot. She handed the mug to Beth.

"You know where to find milk and sugar," she said.

"Sure do," Beth said with a grin. She reached behind her, opened the fridge and poured a dollop of heavy cream into the mug.

She took a sip and then said.

"Who is he?"

"The son of a patient admitted as an emergency."

Why was she avoiding this? Just rip off the band-aid. Nothing had happened, and she doubted Beth would remember Rick.

"The son is Richard Miller. His mother, Frances, was admitted and . . ."

Sue broke off at the wide-eyed surprise on Beth's face.

"What?" she asked.

"No way, that was Richard Miller. He was skinny and shy

and had no coordination. And back in high school, he had one hell of a crush on you."

"What?"

Sue wondered if her speech ability had been reduced to a single word. She reached over and grabbed the chocolate donut before Beth could move the box again. She took a large bite, not caring if the chocolate smeared over her face.

"How do you know?" Sue asked through a mouthful of donut.

Beth rolled her gray eyes, took a sip of coffee, and settled her ample hips against the counter.

"I know because, like everyone else on this planet, I have eyes, and had them back then, long before I needed glasses to read. You only had to see how his eyes followed you. He wasn't a stalker, or anything weird like that, and he tried real hard to hide it."

Sue considered the apple cinnamon, then settled for another bite of chocolate. "How did I not see it?"

"Because you and the real world weren't in the same place those days, Sue. You were so dedicated and focused on becoming a nurse, he could have laid down and declared his love for you, and you wouldn't have noticed."

"He did."

The mug was halfway to Beth's mouth. It shivered and tilted. Coffee spilled down Beth's white golf shirt and splashed onto the floor.

"Shit!"

Sue couldn't keep the giggle inside.

Beth's sour look turned the giggle into a full laugh.

"Payback."

"Now you really have some 'splainin' to do," Beth said as she wiped her front with a paper towel, then used more to dry the floor.

When she was done with the cleanup, Beth refilled her

mug and hopped onto one of the high bar stools under the counter. She patted the stool beside her.

"Come on, Sue. Tell Auntie Beth everything."

Sue swallowed the last of the donut.

She wished she'd kept her mouth shut. Wished she'd stayed in her office last night. Wondered if there was a position at Providence Medical Center in Anchorage. Or Fairbanks.

Something must have shown on her face because Beth's words were softer, caring and compassionate. The way they'd been when she was there for Sue in the days and weeks after Ben died.

"What happened, Sue?"

"Do you remember that Friday night party at the football field the week after we graduated?"

Beth wrinkled her button nose.

"That's asking a lot."

Then her gray eyes sparkled, and she snapped her fingers.

"David Tolliver bought a case of beer. Or was it two? We tried to drink it all. I had half a can and got the hiccups, then I got giggly. Then I threw up. I haven't touched beer since."

"Rick and I were away from the rest of you," Sue said. She ignored the raised eyebrow when she said Rick instead of Richard.

"He told me how he felt. Pretty much what you just said. I told him I didn't feel the same way."

"Best to be honest."

Sue saw the change in Beth's eyes the moment she made the connection.

"Is that why he left town and joined the military?"

The pain and guilt she'd felt last night came back redoubled. The coffee and chocolate soured in Sue's stomach.

For a moment she feared she was going to be ill.

"It certainly didn't help," Sue said when she had her stomach back under control.

"Did you talk about why he left the way he did?"

Sue nodded. "Some. I'm pretty sure there's more. If he wants to share any of it, that's his decision, but you'll not hear anything from me."

Beth considered Sue's words for a moment, sipped her coffee, then nodded. "I get that. Rick suits him from what I hear. Are you going to see him again?"

Sue replayed the coffee conversation from the previous evening in her head. Rick didn't seem to hold a grudge about what had happened. He believed he should apologize to her, even when she told him there was no need.

Sue had liked the easy way the words flowed between them and how they'd laughed together. She couldn't recall when she'd last laughed like that. She was sure it was before Ben died.

Would she see Rick again?

She had spent most of the night tossing and turning with that question rolling through her head.

"Probably at the hospital."

"That's not what I meant, Sue."

She crossed her fingers behind her back. Just in case. "Then, no."

The doorbell chimed.

EIGHT

The thrill of anticipation still bubbled inside Rick as he walked to the drawer at the end of the island. The drawer his mother always referred to as the junk drawer. It was where all the odds and ends were hidden away. Loose change, batteries, spare keys.

Rick was convinced some keys went back to cars he had driven before he joined the Marines.

He pushed everything around in the drawer, not sure what he was looking for until he saw the blue foam float attached to a key ring. He pulled the float free from the clutter and held it in his hand.

Three keys. Gold, silver, and bronze.

Companionway, engine start, and dock gate.

It was like holding a piece of the past.

A past where his parents let him take the Beneteau out into the Gulf before they let him drive.

Rick felt another shiver of anticipation ripple through his body. He picked up the keys to the rental, then dropped them back on the counter. It was a fifteen-minute walk to the marina and one he'd done countless times when he was younger.

Except Diamond Beach had changed.

Rick had been aware of it during his visits home on leave, but in the small subdivision where his mother lived, he'd been shielded. The streets of Florida craftsman homes, with the occasional ranch, had changed little since the 1950s when the concrete block homes were first built.

There had been upgrades. Metal roofs replaced shingles. Garages remodeled into interior rooms, and carports added. Pools were added in the backyard, and mesh screens erected around them.

Rick passed the first screen enclosure three houses down on the opposite side of the road. The pool and enclosure had been built four or five years ago. He smiled at his mother's comments that it looked like a monstrous birdcage.

Mostly the area had escaped the wholesale birdhouse, zero lot line, mega-mansion development he'd seen in other parts of Florida. He was grateful for that. It would have devastated his mother and disoriented him even more than he felt now.

Rick's first challenge came when he reached the road that bisected the island from east to west. The south side of the road had been redeveloped, and everything looked new. The side roads he'd cut through all those years ago to the marina no longer existed or had changed so much he no longer recognized them. In their place were high-end four-story apartments, an expensive-looking hotel, and an area signed as Diamond Beach Wharf.

The hotel he remembered. The Oyster. It bore little resemblance to the elderly, ramshackle, and crumbling building he remembered from his teen years. Someone had spent millions on renovations. The exterior was upgraded and painted in a black-and-white pattern. Turrets had been added to the upper story's and a vast deck with tables, chairs, and umbrellas looked over railings out toward the Gulf.

The double doors to the lobby were propped open and Rick smelled the aroma of fresh coffee, bacon, and truffle oil. For a moment, he was tempted to stop in and try the breakfast advertised on the panels by the doors.

Instead, he walked by.

The siren call of the marina and the Beneteau was stronger than the enticing food smells.

Rick left the hotel on his right-hand side, walked the fifty yards to the entrance to Diamond Beach Wharf. It was a pedestrian area now, with light-colored paving that, even before the sun hit it, seemed to glow and reflect glare. Rick was grateful he'd remembered his sunglasses and guessed that in the middle of a summer day, the Wharf was an uncomfortable place to be.

The wide walkway led to a central square. Well, a hexagon if he was being precise, with a stage, restaurants, stores, and cafes. At this hour, barely seven-thirty, the restaurants and stores were closed and shuttered.

The cafes were open, with tables on the walkway set with cloths, cutlery, and mugs. Early-bird diners were scattered throughout the cafes. Some preferred juice and bagels, others muesli and protein shakes, while the majority chose coffee with eggs, mushrooms, and hash-browns.

Rick's stomach growled as the competing aromas teased him. He'd barely eaten last night in the mad dash to get to the hospital and just had the coffee this morning. Once again, Rick gave thanks he'd been in Jacksonville and not further north at Quantico, or across the country at Twentynine Palms.

He decided that after he'd seen the Beneteau, he'd stop on the way back and treat himself to a full breakfast, and some decent coffee.

What had once been a sandy track along the dunes was now a paved walkway with wrought-iron safety railings, lights at regular intervals and wooden benches where you could sit and watch the waves roll off the Gulf and onto the beach.

Rick paused just short of where the paving became a gravel parking lot. The wind gusted off the ocean, still chilling and able to raise goosebumps on bare arms or legs. Rick was pleased he'd thought to pull a heavy sweatshirt from his bag.

The continual movement of the water soothed him. He hoped the Beneteau wasn't a moldering wreck. It would be good to get out into the Gulf again and worry about nothing more than the wind, the waves, and the set of the sails.

The deep growl of a jet engine pulled Rick back into the present.

He listened for a moment, then turned to the northwest and looked up. Rick lifted his hand to cut the glare in his eyes and studied the brightening early morning sky.

He was out of practice.

It took him a while before he saw the dark silhouette of the F-35.

A single?

Rick's heart thudded harder. He searched the sky for the wingman. Saw nothing, then took a long breath. He wasn't in the Negev. The pilot above him was in friendly skies. Aircraft didn't need to fly in pairs every mission with each pilot looking out for the other.

As the engine growl faded, Rick pushed back from the railing and followed the pathway the last few hundred yards toward the marina.

The gravel of the parking lot crunched under Rick's shoes. A flock of gulls wheeled and squealed over his head. Their cries nearly blotted out the metallic slap-slap of loose halyards against a mast. The sun was just above the horizon, and once again he was grateful for the heavy sweatshirt.

The metal handle of the dock gate was cold to the touch as he pushed the bronze key into the lock and turned. The hinges squealed in protest when Rick pushed the dock gate open.

Three paces and it was like he'd walked into a different world.

The light felt different, less harsh and more pastel. The early morning sun looked brighter, felt warmer. The smell of salt and ozone from the Gulf seemed stronger, and the squeal of the gulls almost musical.

Rick felt something inside him lift away as his shoes thudded on the dock planking to the left turn onto the finger dock and slip F-18.

How many times had he walked these docks, sat in the cockpit of the Beneteau and put his head back into place?

Rick smiled then. Couldn't help himself. Most of those mental resets had been about Sue.

He slowed to a stop as he reached the slip, not sure what he was about to see, afraid he'd find the boat a rotting wreck.

The gel coat had faded from brilliant white to almost pale yellow. Varnished teak glowed in the morning sun. The stanchions and other metalwork were polished to a shine. Rick couldn't see any pitting or oxidizing.

He released a small breath of surprise.

Mama had kept the boat well maintained, and he felt a twinge of guilt that he had expected anything less. His mother was an excellent sailor and, truth told, she had been the one to really teach him the art of sailing and navigation, while has father had taught him how to fix the engine and everything else mechanical.

Both had stood him in good stead during his career in the Marines.

The boat was moored stern to the dock. Rick stepped onto the transom, then up three steps through the swim gate, and ducked his head under the bimini, the blue so faded it was almost white. A heavy canvas cover protected the wheel and navigation display. There were no seat cushions, just the polished strips of teak on the lazarettes.

Rick lifted the cover of the port-side lazarette. Inside were four lifejackets, a Danforth anchor, what looked to be about a hundred feet of line, and a boathook.

As he dropped the cover back into place, a low rumble reverberated across the marina. Two Contender fishing boats rumbled past the end of the dock at slow speed. The slight wake disturbed the still water.

Rick felt the boat rock under him as the heady stink of diesel fumes floated off the Contenders. A flock of gulls followed the fishing boats, squawking, squealing, and flapping their wings. The birds knew that in a few minutes, the Contenders would drop bait into the water to catch bait fish.

He watched the boats rumble out of the marina, past the breakwaters, and out into the Gulf. Rick turned his attention back to the Beneteau and saw the top panel on the companionway hatch was missing.

His first thought was squatters or vandals. Rick reached for the pistol on his right hip, but of course it wasn't there. He hadn't carried a weapon since he got back from the Middle East and the inquiry started.

He let his hand fall away from his hip. There was no visible damage around the hatch, and maybe a logical explanation. If paint and varnish work was being done in the salon, it made sense to keep the inside aired out.

He moved toward the hatch and heard footsteps thumping along the dock.

Rick turned as a lean, sandy-haired man with hazel eyes puffed up to the stern.

"Rick?"

Rick nodded. The man was about his age, his breath clouding in the chill spring air, a hint of red on the tip of his nose. He looked vaguely familiar.

"Mark Wilson," the man said. "You may recall my family owns the marina."

Rick remembered him then. Mark had never been a great academic, but he could craft anything in wood, metal, or fiberglass.

"Still do, I'm guessing," Rick said.

He eased himself around the wheel, stepped down onto the dock and shook the other man's extended hand.

"For the moment. My son Marcus is in the Navy, and Sarah our daughter," Mark shrugged, shook his head, and ran a hand through his thinning sandy hair.

"Sarah's doing work with movie companies. Right now she's somewhere in the Indian Ocean, which is a long-winded way of saying I don't know if this will still be Wilson's Marina in ten years. Maybe less given some of the silly money offers I'm getting. Anyway, you're not here to listen to my whining. What brought you down here this morning?"

"I found your invoice in Mama's mail and came down to see what state the boat was in. She's in much better shape than I expected."

"Frances was sailing her last summer. Not alone," Mark added in response to Rick's sharp look.

"I went with her sometimes, and so did Andrew Jenkins. He's done most of the heavy work on the repairs. You might recall his father. David was a couple of years behind us at school. He got a scholarship to Florida State as a tight end and broke his leg."

"I'll probably recognize him if we meet," Rick said. He hoped so anyway. He doubted everyone looked the same they did at eighteen.

"What does this have to do with the boat?"

"Andrew sleeps on the boat sometimes. Frances knew about it. I came down to warn you."

Several answers rippled through Rick's mind. He settled on one.

As he opened his mouth to speak, a mournful wail of pain and anguish erupted from the cabin.

NINE

The doorbell chimed again.

Beth put her coffee mug on the island, reached for another donut.

"Answer it," Beth said. "Maybe Richard tracked you down."

"Rick," Sue said automatically, then wished she'd stayed quiet.

She slid off the stool, wiped her hands on the back of her jeans and went to the front door.

The silhouette she made out through the frosted glass was too small to be Rick, and she could make out a flowing mane of blonde hair like her own when she was younger. Whoever was there, it certainly wasn't Rick.

In one way, Sue was glad it wasn't him. If he'd searched out where she lived, there'd be a stalker factor to consider. Plus, she wasn't sure she was ready for Beth to meet him and subject him to her relentless questioning.

Sue opened the door, and all thoughts of Rick vanished.

"Emily!" She stepped forward, wrapped her daughter in a

hug. "What are you doing here? Why didn't you come right in? You have a key."

"A surprise weekend visit," Emily said. She returned the hug, then pulled back and gestured at the white SUV in the driveway.

"I didn't recognize the car, so I figured I'd better ring the bell in case you were entertaining. If you know what I mean."

Emily gave a long, suggestive wink that reminded Sue so much of Ben.

There was something about the way Emily spoke, the way her shoulders hunched, and the dark circles round her eyes that made Sue think the humor was overdone and exaggerated for effect.

Something had brought Emily back to Diamond Beach this weekend. Perhaps she just needed a break. Sue doubted it. She had seen the same symptoms on the rare occasions Emily struggled at college.

She'd bring it up later. The front porch wasn't the place to ask those questions.

"It's Beth's car," Sue said, pulling her daughter into the house. "She'll be pleased to see you as well."

"Beth?"

Emily let out a squeal of pleasure that made her sound like a teenager again rather than a woman in her early thirties.

Sue closed the front door, followed Emily back into the kitchen where she and Beth were hugging like they hadn't seen each other in years rather than the three months since Emily had last come home.

There was a part of Sue that felt she should be jealous of the connection Beth had with her daughter. The biggest part of her knew Beth had been the rock Emily relied on after Ben passed, and Sue folded in on herself.

"Why are you here so early?" Emily asked Beth when they

pulled apart, and Emily made a mug of the dark roast she seemed to drink all day.

"Bribing your mother for the truth on a potential man in her life," Beth grinned and pushed the donuts toward Emily.

"A man!"

"As usual, Beth is projecting, dreaming, and exaggerating." Sue said, watching Emily sip coffee, push her blonde hair to one side, and bite into a donut - chocolate desire. That made Sue react.

She leaned forward, snatched the donut from Emily's hand, leaving a trail of chocolate sauce over both their fingers.

"You know better than to steal my favorite. There's maple bacon or blueberry in the box."

"I'll take either, or both," Emily said with a laugh.

Her laugh was a bright, loud, unforced sound that resonated through Sue. How long had it been since she'd heard Emily laugh so naturally and without hesitation?

Emily's laugh stopped.

Sue saw and felt the focus of her daughter's look. Her blue eyes, usually so soft, were now sharp, like sapphire chips; the way they always changed when she concentrated hard on a subject.

"Tell me about him."

Beth opened her mouth to speak.

Emily shook her head. The sapphire sparkled in her eyes. "I asked Mom."

She's enjoying this, Sue thought.

"I hate to disappoint both of you," Sue said. "He's someone Beth and I knew many years ago in high school, and he's back to see his mother, who had a heart attack."

Sue recalled an incident just after Emily started her junior year.

"You know how Diamond Beach works. You have ice

cream with someone new and different, and it's all over town as the newest, biggest, hottest romance."

"Stuart Reese," Emily said with a grimace.

Sue congratulated herself on the deflection. She didn't feel very good about bringing up Emily's high school past, but she needed time to explore, understand, and work out how and why she'd reacted to Rick the way she had.

She didn't want or need Emily or Beth or anyone giving her their views, biases, or opinions.

"Now it's my turn." Sue said. "What brings you here, unannounced? I normally get itineraries and schedules days in advance."

"I needed a break," Emily said, turning back to the counter to refill her coffee.

When Emily's back was turned, Beth frowned at Sue, her reaction confirming what Sue had thought at the front door. They both knew this was unusual.

Sue gave a little shrug.

Beth nodded. She slid off the stool, brushed crumbs off her blouse and jeans.

"I need to get back to Michael. He's got something experimental on the grill. No doubt I'll be expected to help and taste. Will you be here for pizza Monday, Emily?"

"You two still do that?"

"Of course we do. And you're invited, as always."

The disappointment on Emily's face was genuine.

Nothing hidden there, Sue thought as Emily said.

"I have a lunch interview on Monday. Maybe next time when I've sent you schedules and itineraries."

<h1 style="text-align:center">TEN</h1>

*R*ick felt a shiver run down his spine. He'd heard cries like that too often in the last year. He wanted to be certain.

"What happened to Andrew?"

"The Middle East. Same as happened to a lot of the vets around here." David's voice changed then, becoming lower, hesitant, almost apologetic.

"Frances thought you were there as well."

Much as Rick wanted to deny it, there was no sense in avoiding the question. A quick internet search would reveal his name, and probably an image.

"Tel Aviv, Hebron, and the Golan Heights."

Names that had gained very new meanings for every American in the last year.

David gave a slow, measured nod. "I'm told Andrew was in Hebron."

The memories rippled through Rick's mind. A series of harsh, vivid, and brutal vignettes that made him shiver.

"Hebron was ugly," he said, then gestured toward the Beneteau.

"Is there anything we can do for him?"

David shook his head. "Not that I know of. I usually leave him alone until he calms down. You may have better luck. You were there as well and probably have a better understanding than I do. When you're done, we have a restaurant beside the office. It's not as fancy as The Wharf, but the food's good. Our wine selection is one of the best in the Panhandle, but it's a little early for me."

"Me too," Rick said. "Breakfast sounds good though. I'll talk with Andrew, then drop by."

David started to speak, then stopped. Movement in the cockpit of the Beneteau distracted him. Rick followed David's look, saw a young man stumble past the wheel and down to the swim step.

"Morning, Andrew," David said.

There was no response as Andrew stepped awkwardly down onto the dock. His black hair hung in matted clumps around his face. A threadbare gray t-shirt hung loosely on his bony shoulders, a pair of stained denim shorts hung low on his waist, and tattered dock shoes barely protected his feet.

He shivered as the morning breeze ruffled his hair and the t-shirt. Goosebumps blossomed on his bare arms, drawing Rick's attention to the tattoo on the right forearm.

Andrew's head was down, but his brown eyes looked up. He looked at Rick, flicked to David, then back to Rick.

Rick turned to David. "Give us a minute."

"Are you sure?"

Rick's immediate thought was to tell the other man that, of course, he was sure. He wouldn't have asked otherwise. Over the years, he'd learned that snapped, snarled responses rarely got the result he wanted.

Instead, he nodded.

David nodded in return, reluctantly, Rick guessed.

Rick waited until David was back on the main dock, his

footfalls no longer reverberating through the wooden decking.

"I hear you're a Marine."

"Was, Colonel, sir."

It didn't surprise Rick that Andrew knew who he was. Most likely from one of the other vets in Diamond Beach. Maybe even Denson.

"I'm no longer a Colonel, Andrew, but I am a Marine. Did you miss that class at Parris Island?"

Rick smiled inside. It was unlikely. The DIs hammered the once a Marine, always a Marine message into your head every single day.

Head still down, Andrew pulled his arms across his belly as the wind continued to push around them; halyards slapped against masts with an angry, impatient sound. Somewhere along the dock, a soda can rattled and rolled.

"I don't feel like a Marine," Andrew said.

Rick recognized the tattoo now. The mustard yellow castle with a red shield between the towers.

"It happens to all of us at some point, but it changes nothing. You Combat Engineers had it rough in Hebron."

Andrew's head came up now, revealing the livid puckered scar on the right side of his face. His eye drooped down, and the side of his mouth twisted up.

"You have no idea."

His chocolate-brown eyes blazed. The scar seemed to pulse and look more vivid, and his voice was a hoarse scream.

"I was there, son. I know exactly what it was like."

"You can't. You're normal."

Rick laughed then, except it came out more like a manic cackle. He clamped down on the wildness that surged through him before it got out of control.

"You know Gunny Denson?"

A nod of the head.

"Ask him what it was like for the Raiders in Hebron."

And then the idea came to Rick, like it had been hovering in his mind since last evening at the hospital.

"Can you rig a way to get Denson on the boat?"

"He's in a wheelchair. He's got no legs."

"Many people came back from Iraq and Afghanistan and now have prosthetics. That wasn't what I asked."

Something flickered in Andrew's brown eyes. Rick hoped it was attention or interest. At least curiosity.

"Maybe."

Rick pushed.

"Only maybe? I heard Combat Engineers can create anything from nothing."

Rick turned away, felt the change in Andrew. He looked back, saw the young man standing straighter, head up, shoulders back, arms no longer cuddling his belly.

"We can."

Rick gave him a small smile, then used his Colonel voice. "I know you can. And get that haircut. You look like something the Army graduated, not a Marine."

"Sir, yes, sir."

Rick didn't bother to correct him.

The inside of the restaurant was warm and a welcome change from the chill on the dock. There was a counter with six metal stools, and a dozen four-seat tables with red and white checkered tablecloths and worn, but clean and usable silverware. The walls were a faded color that might have been yellow or beige at one time and were mostly hidden by framed photographs of boats and fishermen proudly displaying their catch.

There were six or seven people in the room, sipping coffee, working on their breakfast, or reading something of interest on their phones or tablets.

Where the Wharf was mostly for tourists and visitors, this restaurant was for fishermen and locals.

David sat in the far corner, at the back of a booth, hands wrapped around a steaming mug. He saw Rick and waved him over.

Rick was aware of the turned heads, frowns, and questioning looks as he threaded between the tables and took a seat to David's right where he could see everyone in the restaurant, and the doorway he had just come through.

"Coffee," he said in answer to David's questioning look. "Then I'll have scrambled eggs and crispy bacon."

"Toast? Mushrooms? Tomatoes?"

Rick shook his head, then nodded thanks to the waitress; a young woman with shoulder-length red hair pulled back into a ponytail, freckles dusting her face, and wire-rimmed glasses that made her look like a librarian. She didn't look any older than seventeen or eighteen. She gave Rick a hesitant smile as she slid a chipped white china mug in front of him and filled it from the coffeepot in her hand.

"How was Andrew when you left him?" David asked after the waitress walked away.

Rick considered the question, taking a couple of sips from the mug to give himself a little more time to think.

"We have some shared experiences, and I gave him a problem to solve. I don't know if he'll apply himself to it, but I hope so."

"So do I," David said. "He hasn't exactly been a problem, but he's been a concern. Your mom is one of the few people able to reach through his demons."

"Let's hope she's able to in the future," Rick said.

He shifted back in the seat as his breakfast arrived, let the waitress place the meal before him, and nodded thanks as she refilled his coffee.

Rick was finishing the last of the eggs when he saw movement in the doorway.

Andrew stood there, left hand across his stomach, the other holding the door open.

His t-shirt and shorts looked even more ragged and stained than they had on the dockside. He saw Rick, made a few hesitant steps forward, then seemed to win some internal battle.

His back straightened, his head came up, and he pushed strands of greasy hair off his face.

It wasn't quite a march, but there was a crisp sharpness in Andrew's walk as he came across to the booth, focused on Rick, and not the looks of the other diners. Looks that ranged from distaste, through sympathy to hope.

When he reached the booth, he stopped, not quite at parade rest, but close enough for Rick.

"You were right, sir. It can be done. I need some stuff, and it may take a few days to put it all together."

"I knew you'd find a way, Andrew," Rick said. "Charge anything you need to my mother's account. If anyone questions you, refer them to me."

Even in the lower light at the back of the restaurant, Rick saw the sheen of tears flood into Andrew's eyes. He gave a quick nod, turned away, then paused and looked back.

"And I haven't forgotten the haircut, sir. That's next."

There was a definite change in the young man now. His back was straight, head held high, and he walked with a purpose that hadn't quite been there when he walked into the restaurant.

David's hand was wrapped around his mug, frozen about eight inches off the table, a look somewhere between surprise and disbelief on his tanned face.

After a moment, he came back to himself, and put the mug down.

"I'll have a word," David said to Rick. "Andrew won't encounter any problems."

ELEVEN

*S*ue pushed her office door open and walked in. She pushed a pile of blue report folders aside to make room on the desk for her coffee mug.

Morning sunlight slanted through the blinds, breaking the room into mixed bars of light and shadow.

Mixed, like her feelings, she decided. Mondays weren't normally a chore, but after a weekend with Emily, she was unsettled. It seemed to be a common feeling now whenever Emily left. The feeling that Sue was missing precious time with her daughter, that she was letting the streams of life go by while she drifted in a backwater. There had to be something more to look forward to than this office every weekday morning.

She grimaced when she saw the stacks of folders on her desk. The budget figures absolutely had to be submitted this week, and the staff evaluations - not just her direct reports, but their staff as well.

Sue knew she was late with the budget numbers, late with the operational reports, and late with the evaluations. Her people were also late with the evaluations.

Like her, their passion was helping patients, not completing paperwork.

She sighed to herself. When had it all stopped being enjoyable?

Sue took a sip of coffee, relished the bitter jolt of caffeine and hint of chocolate in the drink.

Setting the coffee down again, she went through the loose papers on her desk, glancing at each one to understand the content, sorting them into piles of similar subjects, and dropping a large percentage into the blue plastic recycle bin beside her desk.

It had been fun when she first got this job. The role was new. The challenge to learn, improve, and succeed. She'd certainly succeeded in all three, she thought as she stacked the blue personnel folders onto a pile of financial reports bound in green.

Now there was space, order and a plan. Budgets first, then evaluations, and finally the operational reports. If she pushed herself and focused, she could have it all done by the end of the day.

Sue dropped into her chair, pulled the keyboard toward her and logged on to the computer.

Her phone rang.

She muttered a curse, thought about ignoring the shrill tone, then saw the caller ID.

She lifted the receiver, making her voice sound cheerful.

"Hi Sarah. How's the ICU this morning?"

"Quiet. Just the way I likes it."

Sarah's lazy Bahamian drawl extended the word quiet into four syllables. Sue smiled, really smiled, as Sarah continued.

"Thought you might like to know your friend from the other night is back."

Sue felt her breath hitch, and her stomach flip partway.

"I'm sure he was here over the weekend as well. How is Ms. Miller?"

"He was, but you weren't."

The teasing humor left Sarah's voice.

"Ms. Frances is holding her own. The cardiologist is coming by later. If it were me, I wouldn't be making any long-term plans."

The warm feeling in her chest became a lead weight in her stomach. Sue hadn't really expected anything else. She had seen it herself and said as much to Rick on Friday.

"Thank you for letting me know, Sarah. Maybe I'll stop by later."

Sue leaned back in her chair, and watched the motes of dust sparkle in the slats of light through the blinds. Each sparkle seemed to be a thought that flickered through her head.

Emily. Ben. Rick.

There was a part of her that wanted to walk upstairs and see him. Another part that felt she would betray Ben by doing so.

And the memory of Ben in those terrible last days, when even Emily had been too upset to visit.

The hospital bed they'd set up in the dining room. The hum, buzz, and beep of the equipment as it monitored his vitals and kept him alive, if you could call it life. The cloying piney scent of antiseptic that made her gag and wonder if she could ever work in a hospital again.

The morning he passed, when he'd reached for her hand, gripped her fingers in his. There was only skin and bone over his fingers, much like Frances, and there was no longer any actual strength in his grip.

"Don't be a hermit," Ben said. "You're beautiful in every way, Sue. Live your life again."

So easy for him to say.

The burst of anger and fury came unbidden, all-consuming and taking her breath away for a moment.

He wasn't the one left to pick up the pieces, deal with the legal issues, and comfort Emily. A daughter, who in many ways was closer to her father than she ever was to Sue.

Sue shook her head, took a sip of the coffee, grateful for the harsh bitter flavor and the heat that scorched her tongue, forced her to focus on something other than memories.

The burst of emotion surprised her. She thought she'd got beyond that, but like the sense of loss and desolation, it still blossomed occasionally, and probably always would.

Sue took another sip of coffee, more to ground and balance herself than because she really needed it

She studied the piles on her desk. At least she had a plan, and the longer she left it, the harder it would be to start.

She pulled the first pile toward her.

Sue ignored the interruptions and spent three solid hours working through the budgets and evaluations. She'd never liked budgets - trying to balance the constraints of what came into the medical center against the costs that left little for programs to help the veterans, people with mental health issues, or those with substance disorders.

Some veterans fell into all three categories.

The budget numbers were abstract, logical, and impersonal.

The evaluations were opposite and very personal.

After five years, Sue knew these people. Some, like Sarah, better than others. They all fell on bell curves of ability, commitment, and attitude.

Six people were at the bottom end of all three. Two of them were already working under performance plans that weren't showing much success. Sue wasn't expected to do the terminations herself, but Diamond Beach was still a small enough community that everyone knew who made the final decision.

As she reached for her mug, Sue wondered how they managed it in the Marines. Probably the same bureaucracy, she thought, and held her hand still as she realized the coffee was cold.

She'd never liked iced coffee, and didn't feel inclined to start now.

It was time for a break, and a fresh mug of coffee.

She made a habit of regularly walking the emergency room, the outpatient areas, and the upper floors with their operating suites, recovery rooms, and the ICU.

No-one would think anything of it if she did one of her walkabouts now.

The delusion lasted until she stepped off the elevator on the ICU floor.

Sarah smiled a welcome, raised her eyebrows at the two cups of coffee Sue carried.

Sue smiled, fought the blush that threatened to color her face, and turned toward the ICU rooms.

The first two rooms were dark and unused, as she expected. In the third ICU room, the lights were on and turned low, to little more than a dull yellow glow.

Sue's first instinct made her glance at the monitors. The red, green, and white lines and numbers flickered and changed on the equipment above Frances's bed.

The numbers, lines and readouts looked normal, or as normal as she'd expect for a woman in her eighties who had suffered a major heart attack.

Rick sat on the far side of the bed, his left hand holding his mother's right hand. On the far side, she noted, where he could watch his mother, the monitors, and anyone coming past the ICU room.

She knew he'd seen her. She lifted the coffee containers, offering one toward him.

His smile gave a glimpse of white teeth, bright in the dim light. Sue saw something spark in his eyes, and his posture relaxed a little.

He leaned forward and kissed Frances on the forehead. Sue saw his mouth move as he said something to her. He released her hand, placed it carefully and gently on the cover, then moved round the end of the bed and out of the room.

"Bless you," Rick said as he came into the hallway and took the coffee from her.

Their fingers brushed, and again, Sue felt the spark flash between them. She felt like that eighteen-year-old on the bleachers, but this time she wasn't scared or afraid.

This time she wanted to explore the possibilities, even though inside she was shaking and quivering with nerves, and a part of her still wondered if she was betraying Ben.

"I wasn't sure you'd still be here."

"Nowhere else to be," he said. He took a careful sip of the coffee, then a longer swallow.

"Thank you. This coffee really is very good." He gestured toward the room. "She seems better today, less restless and not so agitated."

"That may be the medication," she said. "What did the cardiologist say?"

"I haven't seen him yet. The nurse at the station, Sarah?"

Sue nodded.

"Sarah said he's delayed by an emergency. They're expecting him sometime this afternoon."

"Will you be able to wait?"

"I've nowhere else to be," he said with a resigned smile. "It's good spending the time to catch up with Mama, even if only one of us is awake to hear what's being said."

"I had a lot of conversations like that with Ben toward the

end," Sue said, then realized what she'd said, felt her cheeks warm as the flush of embarrassment heated them.

"Oh, Lord. Rick, I'm sorry, I didn't mean to imply."

He put his hand over the one she was using to hold her coffee. It was an unconscious gesture, but it calmed and reassured her all the same. His voice was gentle.

"It's all right, Sue. You were frank with me on Friday, and I've been in enough hospitals this past year that I can interpret the looks and unspoken words. I think your fifty-fifty estimate might be optimistic."

"Or pessimistic," she said, trying to retrieve something. "I was never a cardiology nurse."

"Let's argue that after the doctor's seen her," he said. And then in a rush of words. "Will you have dinner with me?"

She'd had a lot of invitations over the years, declined them all politely and gracefully.

Her automatic reaction was to do the same this time. She drew breath to let him down gently, then recalled her thoughts earlier in the day, and ten minutes ago.

"I'm behind schedule with a lot of paperwork this week. Would Friday work for you?"

Her stomach fluttered with anticipation.

TWELVE

Rick watched Sue walk back to the nurses' station. She walked with slow, graceful elegance that made his mouth dry.

His heart thudded hard. He'd fought hand-to-hand with enemies in the Middle East, and asking this woman on a date felt twice as hard.

Perhaps it was the history between them. Maybe he was off balance because of the inquiry. Maybe he was nervous because he'd asked a beautiful woman on a date.

Not something he did regularly. Rick caught sight of his reflection in the glass window looking into his mother's room, saw the slight smile on his face. He let the smile become a full grin. His friend, Alex would tease mercilessly if he ever found out.

And the surprise was, Rick hadn't really expected her to say yes.

He left the coffee mug on the table outside the room and went back to sit with Frances.

The cardiologist arrived an hour later. He was a short man with a thin face and close-cropped black hair. The name

Smith was woven onto the left breast of his white coat. An entourage of four students and two nurses trailed behind him.

Rick waited in the hallway while they examined Frances. When the examination was complete, they stood in a group at the foot of the bed, engaged in a long conversation. Rick couldn't hear the conversation.

From the way Smith spoke, pointed at a student and waited for a reply, Rick guessed it was a question-and-answer session to test knowledge, process, and understanding of the options available to them.

The session reminded Rick of the after action debriefs during training at Quantico, and later on exercise with the Australian, British, and other European special forces.

When the question-and-answer session was over, Smith dismissed his students and sat in the chair beside Rick. They exchanged pleasantries, then Rick said.

"What are her chances?"

Smith looked surprised at the direct approach. He rubbed the bridge of his nose and pushed his glasses back into place.

It was an unconscious gesture, and Rick wondered how Smith managed that while operating.

"Your mother needs bypass surgery," Smith said, "If I operate today, her chances of survival are very slim. At the moment she is on medication and intravenous nutrients to stabilize her and make her strong enough for the surgery."

"How long will that take?" Rick asked.

Smith shrugged. "At least another three or four days. My inclination is to let her rest and regain strength this week and schedule surgery early next week."

"What are her survival chances next week?"

"She has a strong will," Smith said. "She must have or she wouldn't have survived the heart attack."

He pushed his glasses back into place. "We have the

option of treating your mother with drugs. I wouldn't recommend it. Even with the medication she could have another episode at any time and there are no guarantees she'd get medical help fast enough next time.

"I've reviewed her health records and spoken with her primary care physician. I can't give you specifics, but I'd estimate your mother has a three in four chance of coming through the surgery and having another ten to twenty years of active life."

"Are you asking or telling me?"

Smith gave a weak smile. "Telling you, really. The final decision is your mother's. She's also very capable of making that decision herself. I hope you support whatever she decides."

"I learned a long time ago not to argue with Mama's decisions," Rick said.

He was surprised to see a full, genuine smile transform Smith's face.

"I wish the families of my other patients were as sensible."

Smith reached into the pocket of his coat. His fingers scrabbled with something, then he pulled out a business card. He handed it to Rick.

"I'll be back to see your mother later this week. Talk to her, and if you have questions or concerns. Call me."

Frances was sleeping again when he went back into the room. Rick sat with her, dozing himself until the nurse came in to check vitals.

The noise of the door clicking shut brought him fully awake.

"You should go home and get some proper rest," the nurse said. "She'll need you rested and supportive after the operation."

Rick started to protest, then realized she was right.

"A proper bed is probably better for me than these chairs," he said.

Rick unwound himself from the chair, leaned down and kissed his mother's forehead. Her skin was damp, the skin felt paper thin, and Frances barely stirred.

Outside in the hallway, Rick considered going to find Sue, then remembered the secured doors they'd passed through, and her comment about piles of paperwork.

She'd agreed to have dinner with him. Best not to push his luck.

On the way back to the house, Rick stopped and bought coffee. He brewed a fresh pot, and it tasted as bad as the previous cups.

Rick poured the coffee down the sink, left the pot to drain and walked round the house.

The house felt strange. It hadn't been home for many years but he'd always felt a connection, felt at peace whenever he came back.

Now there was nothing, although that wasn't quite true.

The feeling now was one of not being welcome. Rick had sensed it on Friday evening and again over the weekend. He'd decided it was fatigue from the drive, and worry about Frances.

Now he wasn't so sure.

Rick thought about it for the rest of the afternoon.

The feeling didn't lessen or go away, no matter how much Rick told himself it was all in his mind.

As afternoon turned into evening, Rick didn't think he was going to sleep at all well here. His stomach growled, a reminder he'd eaten very little today, and that made the decision easier.

Rick slung his bag over his shoulder, locked the house and drove to the Oyster Hotel for dinner and a bed.

THIRTEEN

At five-thirty, Sue did something she rarely did.

She shutdown her laptop, grabbed her jacket from the hook behind the door and went home.

All the paperwork was complete and submitted, and she'd spent time with one of the underperforming employees.

That had been a difficult conversation, but worthwhile. Sue had a much better insight into the personal challenges the young man faced. Fortunately, there was an open position that better suited his abilities, and the last thing Sue had done was to submit the paperwork.

She knew she should be happy, or pleased, or at least satisfied with her accomplishments for the day.

Instead she felt flat, and drained, and not at all in the mood for her Monday pizza outing with Beth.

Sue dropped her purse on the kitchen counter, then went upstairs and took a long shower. She hoped the hot water would wash away her funk.

It didn't.

As she rummaged through her purse for her phone so she could call Beth and cancel, the doorbell rang.

Beth wasn't accepting any excuses.

"This is why we get together on Monday evenings. It has a one in five chance of being the worst day of the week. I think it's higher than that because everything that didn't get done on Friday bubbles and ferments and festers over the weekend, then bursts on Monday."

She pushed the open purse toward Sue.

"Come on. You're getting out of the house this evening. Everything that's bothering you will still be there tomorrow. After a couple of glasses of wine and a good night's sleep, you'll see things differently in the morning."

"I doubt that," Sue said.

She picked up her bag and followed Beth out into the driveway where she strapped herself into the passenger seat and watched.

It didn't take long for Beth to speak.

"Would you object if we do wings at the Marina?" Beth asked as she reversed back down Beth's driveway.

"Mike cooked pizza on the grill last night, and I need to at least pretend to watch my weight."

Sue clipped her seat belt in place, leaned back against the headrest, and tried to suppress the smile that came automatically at Beth's words.

"I've eaten nothing today but junk and protein bars that taste like sawdust. Honey mustard wings sound great."

Beth made a face as she shifted into drive. "We need to get you eating food with real flavor, not that strange Yankee stuff you learned in Baltimore."

"You leave Baltimore alone," Sue said.

It was an old argument between them, and usually Sue had more passion and vehemence in her defense of the Charm City. Tonight, she didn't have the energy, passion, or enthusiasm for the banter.

She had finished the paperwork by early afternoon. It was

a chore that left her eyes sore, head hurting, and shoulders tense from being hunched over the keyboard for several hours without a break.

Sue hadn't intended to walk the halls again. Certainly hadn't intended to visit the ICU and expose herself to Sarah's assessing and speculative gaze.

Fortunately, Sarah was on a break.

Unfortunately, Rick had left.

The feeling of disappointment that twisted her stomach and left a hollow ache surprised Sue when she learned he wasn't there.

"Bad day?" Beth asked as the wheels crunched on the gravel parking lot at the Marina.

Sue realized she'd been lost in her thoughts for the past five minutes of the drive and hadn't said a word.

"Kinda," she said. "It's budget, assessment, and review time. You know how much I love all the paperwork and bureaucracy."

Beth made a gagging sound as she came round the car and looped her arm over Beth's shoulders.

"It's a good job you're not driving and David stocks some superb Italian reds."

"We'll see about that," Sue said as they pushed through the doors. "I still have to work tomorrow."

They pushed through the door and into the pleasant chill of the air-conditioned interior.

Wing night was well known to the locals in Diamond Beach. The tables were full of families or small groups. The stools at the bar were fully occupied, and Beth made a sour face as the hostess approached.

"We're out of luck at the bar," Beth said. "Table or booth?"

"Booth," Sue said to the red-haired hostess, then to Beth. "We can talk there without shouting."

They followed the hostess across the room to the last

booth tucked in a corner right beside the bar. Sue let her nostrils and taste buds revel in the odor of freshly cooked fries, truffle oil, and the various spices and rubs used on the wings.

She smelled garlic, onion, and paprika, and rethought her earlier decision about honey mustard.

As they settled themselves in the booth, Beth said to the hostess. "If you still have any, can we get two glasses of the Montalcino?"

The young woman smiled, and her wire-rimmed glasses flashed in the light.

"You're in luck," she said. "We had a delivery this morning."

"What did you just order for me?" Sue asked as she pulled a paper napkin from the holder on the table and wiped away a damp spot.

"Montalcino," Beth said. "Mike calls it a baby Brunello."

"Like Nebbiolo is a baby Barolo?"

Beth smile was wide and ecstatic. "You're learning. When are you seeing Rick next?"

"Friday for dinner."

Under the table, Sue clenched her fist in frustration at the lapse. She had promised herself she'd say nothing about Rick. She hadn't worked through the feelings swirling in her head, and here they were, barely sat down and Beth had teased the information from her.

Maybe she should skip the wine and go straight to water or there'd be no telling what else revealed.

Beth was shaking her head in wonder, chestnut curls bouncing from side to side.

"You must be distracted. I figured it would take at least one glass of wine to crack you. Maybe even two."

"I planned on you learning nothing," Beth said with a

rueful smile, then nodded her thanks to the hostess as their wine arrived.

"You should know me better than that. Now try the wine and tell me everything else. What made him ask you? And what made you say yes?"

Sue took Beth's advice. She lifted the glass, swirled the wine a little and took a small sip. She tasted cherry and blackberry, and underneath hints of espresso. The wine flowed smoothly over her tongue and she swallowed without tasting the bitter, tangy bite of tannins.

"It's good," Sue said, and took another sip. "What are you ordering?"

"Chipotle pineapple and sriracha. Where's he taking you for dinner?"

"He didn't say. I think he has somewhere like the Oyster in mind."

Beth raised her eyebrows. "Impressive."

She broke off to order her wings, then raised her eyebrows once more when Sue said.

"I'll have the chipotle pineapple and chili lime."

"Who are you, and what did you do with my friend?" Beth asked, but Sue didn't miss the sparkle in Beth's eyes.

"I have a better idea for your evening out, if you're up for it."

Sue took another sip of the Montalcino. It really was very smooth and very good.

"What do you mean?"

"Have dinner with us. I'll have Michael put ribs on the grill. Besides, I want to meet Rick again before the rest of the town does."

Sue drew a breath, ready to argue until she saw the look on Beth's face. The tight white line of her lips. The uncompromising look in her chocolate brown eyes. The way Beth sat hunched forward at the table.

Sue had fought battles like this with Beth in the past.

She'd lost every one of them.

"Only if he agrees," Sue said. She reached for her phone and dialed Rick's number as Beth sat back, a satisfied smile on her face

"It's me," she said when Rick answered. "Can we take a rain check on dinner? My supposed friend Beth believes you need to be checked out before I'm allowed to appear with you in public."

His chuckle was warm and near. It felt like he sat right beside her, and without thinking, Sue shifted a little to her left to be close.

"That's fine," Rick said. "We'll talk tomorrow or the day after and work out what I can bring and when I pick you up."

When she hung up, Beth was watching her over the rim of her wine glass.

"What?"

Beth smiled. A big satisfied smile like a cat who stole the cream.

"You are lost. You don't know it yet. Not really know it, and I can't tell you how happy that makes me."

Sue had a feeling Beth was right, but she wasn't giving her the satisfaction of knowing it. Instead, Sue just smiled and sipped from her wineglass.

FOURTEEN

On Friday evening, Rick pulled on a pair of khakis, a flowered silk shirt, and deck shoes. He was, he admitted to himself, more than a little nervous. It was one thing to take Sue out on her own. Completely different to meet her friends at their home.

As he pulled into Sue's driveway, he heard the deep rumble of Pratt and Whitney turbofan engines. Instinctively, he looked up but there was just enough cloud and haze, he couldn't see the F-35's. A pair though. He was sure of that.

Sue opened the door as he reached it. She'd let her strawberry blonde hair, hang in a soft wave around her face, and down onto her shoulders. A peach camisole top with spaghetti straps, and white hip-hugging capri's completed her wardrobe.

"You like?" She asked, a smile brightening her face.

Rick felt himself flush. "Was I staring?"

"A little, but I'll forgive you as it does my ego good."

"Then I'll keep doing it until you tell me it's creepy," he said, as he opened the car door for her.

"Help me not to make a complete idiot of myself," Rick said as he reversed down the driveway.

"Should I remember Beth and Michael from school?"

"Not Michael," Sue said, settling into her seat. "He came to Diamond Beach two or three years after you left. He worked at the marina for a while, met Beth and the rest, as they say, is history."

Rick made a connection in his head. "Beth whose mother should have been a chef?"

Sue couldn't hold back a laugh that bubbled up. "Typical man. Never mind that she was an award-winning artist and founded the Diamond Beach Art Festival. All you remember is her cooking."

"It was pretty good cooking," Rick said. He remembered the pasta dishes with the nutty smell of shredded parmesan, and the spicy, peppery scent of fresh basil.

"Don't expect too much tonight. That gene mostly skipped right by Beth. Michael though, Michael is good with the grill. My guess is we're getting ribs with beans and hash browns."

Rick kept his face neutral.

As a junior officer, he'd attended many barbecues and cookouts hosted by Majors and Colonels, all of whom considered themselves gifted at smoking meat.

Few lived up to the expectations.

Mentally, he prepared himself for dried meat, burned potatoes, and overly spiced beans.

The GPS beeped at him. Rick made the right turn and pulled up at the security gate. The gate was ornate scroll-work painted white with gold lettering that spelled out Diamond Beach Golf and Country Club.

"I'm guessing Michael isn't a marina worker any longer."

"He never was," Sue said. "He was taking a year after his degree to decide whether to study for a Master's degree, then got recruited by a finance company. Beth calls him a finance geek. If you let him, Michael can talk for hours about alphas and Greeks and something called iron condors."

"A pretty successful geek, I imagine," Rick said, braking to a stop at the guard house.

They showed their driver's licenses to the security guard. Rick was pleasantly surprised to learn he'd been added to the approved visitor list.

As he drove through the open gate, Rick vowed not to read too much into it. He could be removed as easily as he'd been added.

They stopped twice to allow carts with golfers to cross the road before Sue gestured at a lane on the right.

"Down there," she said. "Fourth house on the left."

The house was midway along the cul-de-sac. It was a two-story colonial with four cream colored concrete columns that contrasted with the red brick exterior and terracotta barrel tile roof. The columns supported a covered porch that drew the eye to a huge arched double door with a mahogany surround and leaded windows that reflected the low sun in a cascade of rainbow colors.

Rick parked before the triple garage. When he got out of the car, cradling the bottle of wine he'd bought, he smelled charcoal, the odor of meat cooking, and something else. It took him the time to walk round the car and help Sue out before he recognized the smell. Cherry.

His hopes for the food this evening lifted a notch.

A trio of cameras on the garage and over the porch watched them as they walked side by side along the paved walkway. Sue walked close beside Rick. Her shoulder not quite brushing his upper arm. He caught the fragrance of her perfume, a delicate combination of peaches and mangoes that almost masked a deeper woodsy citrus scent.

The scent that was Sue, that instinctively he knew was how she'd taste and smell as he ran his mouth over her body.

Rick turned his head a few degrees, took a long breath in the hope he'd inhale more of the wood smoke and less of Sue. Something. Anything to distract himself and ease the tightness in his khakis.

Sue eased easily in front of him and the front door swung open before she reached for the bell push.

A door bell with a camera, Rick noted approvingly.

Rick stood to one side as the two women hugged, then allowed himself to relax as Beth wrapped her arms round him. She was about the same height as Sue, but heavier and with more pronounced curves. Up close she smelled of pepper, garlic, and lemon.

"I doubt you remember me, Rick," Beth said as she released him and flipped her hand through locks of rich chestnut hair. "This used to be mouse brown, and I was as skinny as Sue still is, and I should hate her for it. You've gained weight as well, and I know it looks better on you than me."

He'd remembered her name, but couldn't place her, really place her until now. Her breathless, rapid pace of talking. The words bubbling and spilling out of her mouth as her hazel eyes sparkled.

Rick imagined this was how champagne would sound if it could talk.

Beth closed the door and ushered them through the house into the huge chef's kitchen with granite countertops, stainless appliances, and a view out across an extensive patio toward a golf green where a pair of golfers were sizing up their putts.

"I'd never forget your voice," Rick said, offering the bottle of wine he carried.

"I'll assume that was a compliment," Beth said, her hazel

eyes still twinkling as she glanced at the label on the bottle, then back to Rick.

"Barolo. Did you get some inside information?"

"Sue was kind enough to offer some suggestions."

"I'm sure," Beth said with a mischievous grin. "Michael will love this."

"What will Michael love?" Asked a deep voice with a hint of Boston or Rhode Island.

A door banged closed, and a man came in on the far side of the kitchen. Rick estimated he was two or three inches taller than Rick's six feet. And lean, almost too thin although Rick sensed a deep strength in the man.

Michael had thinning sandy hair, piercing blue eyes and a full mouth that looked like it spent most of the time smiling.

Michael wiped a hand on the blue-gray grilling apron, stepped forward, and offered his hand.

Michael's grip was firm without trying to get into the finger-crushing contest so many men tried when they first met Rick.

He appreciated that.

"It's good to meet you, Rick. Grab a glass of whatever you're drinking and join me on the deck. No interrogations, I promise. That's Beth's department."

"Michael!"

"You know he's right," Sue said. She turned back to Rick, laughter in her blue eyes. "Wait until those soft hazel eyes harden up, and that voice you remembered becomes as sharp as a boning knife. She keeps at it until you have no option but to confess."

"Sue! You're supposed to be my friend."

"Which is why I can tell it how it is," Sue said.

She walked around the counter, kissed Beth on the cheek as she passed. She pulled two glasses from the glass-fronted cabinet with the familiarity of someone who spent a lot of time at the house, and was a welcome and valued guest, or honorary family member.

Rick felt a twist in his stomach as she poured two glasses of red wine. He'd never stayed anywhere long enough to establish and build those connections and friendships.

For a long time he'd told himself it didn't matter.

Now he wasn't so sure.

He took the glass from Sue, wondering if he imagined it, or if her fingers stayed on his hand a beat or two longer than necessary.

That way led to madness.

Rick pushed the thought out of his head and followed Michael out onto the deck.

FIFTEEN

The door closed with a click. Sue heard the low rumble of the men's voices on the other side. Beth walked over, pushed at the door with her shoulder to make sure it was fully closed.

"He still looks at you the same way."

Sue let out a laugh that was almost a snort.

"You're working on a dream, Beth. I don't remember half of what I did twenty years ago, and you expect me to believe your memory of an event where you spent half the evening throwing up, is perfect."

Beth smiled, and her hazel eyes twinkled.

It was a smile Sue knew too well. In this mood, Beth's version of reality was the only one that existed.

"That evening at the bleachers, you're right. I'm talking about all the other times I mentioned before. There are some things that stick in your mind. That's one of them. There's also the day David Wilson took a running dive off the dock and lost his swim shorts."

Sue had the glass almost to her mouth and moved it away as she laughed again.

"Oh, yes. That I remember. I don't think I've ever seen anyone look so mortified, before or since."

David's dive had been the Easter before graduation. One event in a long summer that Sue always remembered fondly, even when most of the specific things that happened were no longer recalled.

"We had some good times that year, didn't we?"

"Past tense?" Beth looked offended. "You've had good times since then. They were just different, and you can have them again if you accept you don't have to live the life of a hermit."

"I am not a hermit."

Beth wagged her finger as she took a sip of wine. "Yes, you are. You only go out with Emily or me. When did you last go to a leaving party for someone at the medical center?"

"My presence makes everyone unsettled. They're not comfortable seeing the boss on those evenings."

Even to Sue's ears, the excuse sounded lame.

This time, Beth's voice was softer, gentler, more sympathetic. "That's not the reason, Sue. Not the real one."

Sue was never comfortable when Beth turned from friend and confidante to counselor. They knew each other too well, better in some ways than Ben had known her.

Beth knew the location of all the dark nooks and crannies inside Sue's mind. The places where she hid or ignored things she didn't want to remember or talk about.

This was another of those times when she couldn't avoid the conversation.

"It's the couples," Sue said as she twirled the stem of the glass between her fingers.

"More often the men. Even though they know about Ben, there's a word, or a look or a gesture that has me thinking I'm being judged for being single."

She took a sip of the wine. The peppery taste of the

Barolo was almost too sharp for her. She put the glass down on the granite counter, ran her hand through her hair, not caring that the careful patting and primping from earlier dissolved into a tumble of wisps and curls.

"It's not that I haven't had invitations. I haven't been interested."

Beth eyed her over the rim of her wineglass. The pepper taste clearly wasn't too sharp for her.

"And now?" Beth asked, "With Rick?"

Sue shook her head, moved round the counter, so she had something to do, some action to take before she had to answer. There were more golfers on the green; a party of four this time. To her left, she saw Rick and Michael chatting amiably.

Something twisted in her chest.

"He feels safe," she said.

"Safe because he'd do anything for you, or safe because he's likely not going to be here long term?"

The two extremes.

Sue had bounced between them in her mind, like a never-ending tennis rally.

"I'm not sure," she said finally.

Beth had followed her around the counter. She wrapped her arms around Sue, and Sue smelled the lemon, pepper, garlic scent that was Beth.

"You're overthinking it," Beth said softly in Sue's ear. "I stand by what I said on Monday evening. Part of you already knows. The rest of you just needs to catch up."

Like she'd done on Monday, Sue smiled and took a sip of her wine. She still wasn't sure which parts of her were catching up.

SIXTEEN

Rick heard the door click closed behind him, then a few beats later, a more solid thud as the latch caught.

The deck ran the full length of the back of the house. The maple-colored synthetic wood felt solid under Rick's feet. To his right, a circular wrought-iron table was shaded by a faded white umbrella and surrounded by six chairs. Pots of roses, magnolias, and yellow-flowered plants Rick couldn't identify ranged in clumps in front of the wooden rail work that ran waist-high around the edge of the deck.

Michael waved toward a pair of wooden chairs that faced a dark-green kamado grill and also gave a view of the green where the golfers had replaced the flag and were walking away to their golf-cart.

"I don't really need to babysit the ribs," Michael said as he settled himself into one of the chairs.

"I spend most of the day in front of computer screens in the office upstairs and rarely get away for anything except a bathroom break or more coffee. It feels good to sit out here and get some air, even in August and September when you can chew the humidity."

Rick was feeling better about dinner.

He had glanced at the temperature gauge on the upper slope of the dome. Two hundred and seventy, or maybe eighty, Fahrenheit. The smell of the rib meat coming through the upper vent with faint curls of clear smoke made his mouth water.

"I know that feeling," Rick said as he eased himself down into the chair, felt the slats bite into his shoulder blades.

"You seem to have a good handle on what's happening with the meat."

Michael took a sip of his wine. "That's easy," he said.

"It's easy if you pay attention. Get the coals to about two-seventy-five, give the ribs two hours, then wrap them in foil and wait another hour."

He glanced at the bulky gold-colored watch on his left wrist. "Another twenty minutes and I'll take them off and let them sit for half an hour.

"I'm sorry to hear about your mom. I've not met her, but Beth has talked about her a lot, especially in the past week. Have the doctors said anything about further treatment?"

Rick shook his head, took a sip of his own wine and let the spicy, licorice flavor wash over his tongue. A Barolo, and a very good one. He offered a prayer of thanks for Sue's advice and said.

"I spoke with the consultant on Monday, and again yesterday. He believes her body is now strong enough to survive the surgery, so unless anything changes, the surgery is scheduled for next Wednesday."

Rick took another sip of wine and watched a foursome arrive on the green. The young men tumbled out of the carts, laughing, joking, and trading insults as they selected clubs and made their way into the bunker that guarded the front of the green, or onto the green itself.

They watched the first golfer spray sand as he chipped out of the bunker, across the green and into the rough on the far side.

Then Michael said. "How long are you planning on being here?"

Rick was tempted to challenge him about interrogations, but it was a reasonable question.

"I'm not sure," he said. "A lot depends on Mama and her recovery. There are meetings at the Pentagon I may have to attend as well. After that, it depends where I'm posted, unless I put in my papers."

And with a chance the next posting could be a cell at Leavenworth, he'd deliberately avoided making any plans.

"Will you put in your papers?"

"There are some things to sort out first. It's probably the first option," Rick said. "I'm at the top end of the age for a Colonel, and I'm not seeing any Generals retiring."

"Sorry," Michael said, as the first of the golfers holed out accompanied by derisive cheers. "I promised no interrogation, and here I am doing just that."

"I'm used to it," Rick said, then changed the subject. "How long have you had the kamado?"

"Fifteen years," Michael said. "I was replacing my gas grills about every eighteen months. A friend told me this would be the last grill I'd ever buy. So far he's been right."

A buzzing noise cut across their conversation. Michael twisted in his seat, pulled his phone and stabbed buttons with his fingers.

"Ribs are ready," he said, and handed Rick his wine glass. "If you bring that and hold the door, I'll deal with the ribs."

With the ease gained through regular practice, Michael lifted the dome of the grill, used mitts to transfer three foil packages onto a rectangular platter, and closed the upper and lower vents.

Rick held the door for Michael and saw that one of the foil packs had split open. Inside was a slab of ribs covered with a rub so dark it was nearly black. Some of the meat had fallen away from the bone, revealing juicy strips of meat with a salmon-colored smoke line. The aroma was rich, earthy, and moist.

Rick felt his mouth water, and his concern about the food shifted from concern to anticipation.

Inside, Beth and Sue had set places on the island, and mingling with the smell from the ribs came beans, hash-brown potatoes, and sweet corn.

"What are you treating us to tonight?" Sue asked as Michael laid the plate of ribs on a trivet.

Michael pointed to each foil package as he answered.

"Ancho cocoa, cherry chipotle, and my Bobby Flay variation."

"Variation?" Rick asked.

The three of them looked at him with knowing smiles.

"I used a standard combination of ingredients from a Bobby Flay grilling book. It seemed a little bland to Beth and me, so I added some habanero powder to kick it up a bit. The other two are milder, if spicy isn't your thing."

"I'll try them all," Rick said, and he did.

The conversation as they ate was easy and full of laughter. Beth asked her questions without getting into full interrogation mode, although Rick saw a glance pass between her and Sue on more than one occasion.

He felt welcomed, included, and part of something, although what that was, he couldn't quite place.

It was nearly midnight when he and Sue left the house. Rick had sipped one more glass of wine after the first, aware it was summer, and the Diamond Beach Police Department had a policy of zero tolerance.

A DUI wouldn't help his case with the Pentagon.

Rick pulled the rental car into Sue's driveway and was out and around the car to open her door, to help Sue out.

The surprise and pleasure in her emerald eyes was worth the effort and made his pulse jump.

"You don't have to walk me to the door."

Rick heard the protest in her voice, but it was half-hearted. There was an undertone of surprise and pleasure as well.

Rick was glad he'd made the effort.

She punched the numbers on the digital keypad, and while he tried not to look, the beeping tones resonated in his mind - one nine nine two seven two five. The numbers obviously made sense to her, but would be hard for someone to guess.

As she pushed the door open, Rick leaned forward to tell her goodnight, and to kiss her cheek.

Sue turned toward him.

Their mouths collided.

SEVENTEEN

The attraction that had smoldered since the previous Friday in the hospital erupted into something emotionally real, and physical, and no longer able to be denied.

Sue's senses swirled around her.

She had turned to say goodnight or ask if he wanted coffee or a nightcap.

She tasted the Barolo on Rick's breath. She inhaled the musky, piney scent that was uniquely Rick.

She felt him stiffen, his body become still, like he was unsure of the next move. Ready to pull back.

Too soon, Sue told herself.

Too soon.

Was it really?

She had dated no one since Ben. Never had the interest, motivation, or desire.

Rick though.

He wasn't the skinny, hesitant, half-man she'd rejected all those years ago.

This Rick was muscled, confident, and knew what he wanted.

She shivered at the knowledge that right now, what he wanted was her. Shivered again as she realized she absolutely had desire, motivation, and interest where Rick was concerned, whatever she'd told Beth.

Sue curled her hand into the front of his shirt, leaned into him, and let her tongue run across his lower lip.

There was a deep, low noise from his throat, like a growl or a warning but laced with need and desire.

Sue felt his left arm slide around into the small of her back. His right hand cradled the back of her head. His fingers sifted through her hair as his tongue teased, probed, and demanded.

Maybe all her parts were catching up with each other.

Reluctantly, she pulled her mouth away from his.

"You need to come inside or Mrs. Callahan across the street will have her drapes twitching."

Sue felt the rumble of his chuckle deep in his belly; a belly molded hard against her abdomen.

Another shiver.

Sue felt the arousal deep and low in her body, felt the dampness between her thighs, and was glad she had worn a loose flowing skirt.

She stepped back, reached for Rick's hand and squeezed it hard.

"Inside," she said, and pulled him after her.

Rick's hands on her waist guided them carefully into the hallway. He used his foot to push the door closed, then turned her to face him.

The look on his face was serious, concerned, and slightly hesitant. Sue hadn't seen that hesitancy before. Not even when they were eighteen.

"Is me being here like this going to be a problem for you?"

It took a few seconds for Sue to understand his meaning.

At that moment, she fell a little in love with him.

Sue took Rick's hand, led him down the hallway, into the combined kitchen and family room. She leaned against the smoky gray granite island and slipped her hands around his waist.

"I bought this house a year after Ben died. We had a place in Mack Bayou over in Walton County. Much as I loved the house, every room reminded me of Ben. It was like he was still there. I know people who take comfort in that and can live and thrive in the house they shared with a spouse who passed. It had the opposite effect on me."

"What happened?"

"I wasn't answering emails, my phone, or texts. Beth came over to check and found me alternately screaming and crying, and in the middle of a first-class meltdown. She dragged me out of the house, and I stayed with her and Mike for nearly a month before I sold the place and came here. My daughter, Emily wasn't happy with me until Beth talked to her."

She looked up at him. His blue eyes were full of compassion, with a bright sheen that looked like tears.

"Am I making any sense?"

"More than you know," he said. "I was fine at Mama's house until two nights after I arrived, and then it felt alien, strange and wrong. I've been back during the day and it's okay, but at night."

He shivered.

"You're not staying there now, are you?"

Rick shook his head. "I have a room at the Oyster while I work out what needs to be done in the house when she comes home."

She nodded, feeling relief that he was away from the house. "That's probably a smart move. I should have done something similar much sooner."

She moved her hands again, slid them up under the soft silk of his shirt, feeling the contrast of hard, corded muscle up his back.

"Now we've got that out of the way, will you please kiss me again?"

His mouth was on hers almost before the words were out.

They danced a lover's dance. A slow waltz of nuzzling, nibbling, and tiny passionate bites as his shirt and her top drifted to the floor.

Arms still locked around each other, Sue led him along the hallway, into her bedroom. A tango this time. Faster, needier, and increasingly urgent.

Her skirt and bra, his khakis and boxers were stripped away.

Sue lay back on the soft, enveloping warmth of the duvet. She reveled in the way his mouth caressed her nipples. His fingers trailed across her belly, sending fluttering sensations into her stomach and warmth into her core.

His hand drifted lower, to the lace band at the top of her panties.

She tensed.

His hand froze in place. He lifted his head.

"What's wrong?"

The first words either of them had spoken in ten minutes.

Sue was grateful for the half-light. Grateful, he couldn't see the heat burning her face. She squeezed her eyes shut, focused on keeping her voice normal, which was a challenge as his thumb had unfrozen, and circled over her belly, leaving swirls of heat like a branding iron.

"It's been a long time since I slept with anyone, Rick. Ben

and I didn't make love for at least a year before his diagnosis. There's been no-one since."

She paused as he shifted, moving up beside her on the bed, his head on his left elbow as his right hand gently caressed her cheek.

"If it's too soon, just say so. It's okay."

She shook her head, nestling her cheek against the rough calluses on his palm and fingers.

"It's not that. I want you, and I want you tonight. What I'm trying to say is that maybe don't expect too much."

"You'll be fine," he said. "It will all come back to you, just like riding a bike."

"Well, that's really going to be a problem because I never learned to ride a bike."

He had leaned over, presumably to kiss her, and her words brought an explosion of laughter. She smelled the warmth of his breath, still rich with the Barolo they'd drunk, wash over her face, and then she was laughing, and coughing, and had to sit up.

His arm went around her shoulders, and she snuggled into his side as they leaned back on the pillows that cushioned them from the headboard.

"I think we lost the moment," he said, but there was still humor in his tone.

Sue felt relief wash through her that he wasn't upset or repelled.

She slipped her arm around his waist, felt the hard ridge of a scar just under his rib cage.

"You'll still stay, won't you?"

She felt his head move, felt the brush of his kiss on the top of her head.

"I'd like that."

Sue hadn't expected to fall asleep so easily, especially with

Rick's hard, muscular body spooned against hers, his right arm hooked over her waist, fingers splayed over her belly.

There was no light in the bedroom when Sue woke. The heavy drapes kept the light at bay. She guessed it was four, maybe five in the morning.

Rick remained curled behind her, holding her close, his right hand now cupping her breast.

And he wasn't snoring.

It was a pleasant surprise, even as Sue tempered the feeling with the memory that Ben hadn't snored until after they were married. Then it had been four nights out of five. Nine of ten sometimes.

She allowed herself a smile. Better to take what she had than set expectations, and who knew if they'd ever have another night together.

The smile made Sue stretch her back. She did it without thinking, her back elongating, her bottom pushing against Rick's groin. She felt the heat flush through her body as he shifted, his breathing changing, his early morning erection building, growing, thrusting against her as it became bigger.

The fingers that cupped her breast flexed, curled, and shifted. She felt the pad of his thumb brush her nipple. It was like a small electric shock that ripped through her body, down through her belly, and into her core.

"You awake?"

His voice was low, muffled by her hair, still heavy with sleep.

"Yes."

The murmur was barely past her lips when she felt his head move. His nose pushed her hair aside. His lips touched her neck in the soft place just below her ear. He paused there for a while, then trailed soft kisses down her neck to her shoulder.

There was a low, desperate noise in Sue's head, then she

realized it came from her mouth, followed by a whimper as Rick nibbled his teeth along the length of her collarbone.

She shifted, twisted, and turned so they were face to face.

"Very awake," she said.

Sue felt the warmth of his breath on her cheek, felt his body move so his face was in front of her, a dark blue in the darkness.

She stretched up toward him, as he lowered and captured her mouth, his tongue jousted with hers as he pushed in, claiming her.

He rolled her until she was on her back, half under him. His right knee nudged her legs wide, and he settled there. His hard length, slick with pre-cum nudged against the slick wetness of her folds.

Sue expected to feel nervous, self-conscious, even a little scared.

Instead, she was calm, more than comfortable with who she was, and yes, very aroused.

She realized Rick had stopped moving.

"Rick?"

"Are you sure?"

Damn him for being overly considerate.

She shifted her hips, a move she'd read in one of Nora's books, and always wanted to try. Sue reached down, her arms just far enough to get her hands under his butt. She pulled, and he slid inside.

His gasp of surprise was almost a chuckle, but Sue didn't really hear it. She focused on the way he stretched her, filled her, sent tingles and sensations spearing through her body.

She hooked her legs around his thighs, pulled him in deeper and let the wonderful sensations course, pulse, and ripple through her body.

"Sue."

The passion and emotion in that one word broke something inside Sue. She shifted her arms, wrapped them around his broad shoulders, felt the ripples and undulations of more scar tissue under her fingers.

A conversation for another time.

She hugged him close, felt the wiry curls on his chest brush and further inflame her nipples.

"Love me, Rick," she whispered in his ear. "Love me."

EIGHTEEN

*R*ick rolled over, stretched his back and felt two of his lower vertebrae click as he did so.

There was a moment of disorientation. The firmness of the mattress. The sheet that slid softly off his shoulders when he moved, rather than scraped like the sheets in the hotel. And the soft scent of magnolia and roses that you definitely didn't find in a hotel bedroom.

He stretched again and smiled as the same two vertebrae clicked again. Only two? The energy and exercise he and Sue had spent in the past week had most of his joints creaking, but creaking in a good way.

He sensed without opening his eyes that the other side of the bed, Sue's side, was empty. Rick stretched out a hand, felt the sheets still warm.

When he opened his eyes, there were narrow bars of light coming through the blinds. The door to the en-suite bathroom was ajar, and the short satin robe Sue wore in the morning was missing from the hook on the back of the door. He could smell the faint scent of her fragrance and heard movement from the kitchen along the hallway.

After that first night a week ago, Sue had insisted he stay with her.

It surprised him, scared him a little, how easily they'd fallen into a routine together.

And how Beth and Michael had accepted him.

Rick was grateful for that acceptance. He wasn't sure where he and Sue were headed. He didn't think she knew either, and was working on the same amount of faith and crossed fingers.

Rick still hadn't told her about the hearings at the Pentagon. The right moment never seemed to present itself. Although the uncertainty ate at him, Rick was content to listen to Alex's assurances that all was going well and there would be no lasting problems.

Easy for Alex to say. Alex had his family and its connections to fall back on. Rick smiled again as he swung his legs out of bed and headed for the bathroom.

Alex had never used those connections, even when it could have got him a comfortable desk in the Pentagon far away from the chaos, murder, and mayhem of the Middle East.

The longer Rick left telling Sue the full story, the more likely she'd believe he'd been hiding everything from her.

I'll tell her tonight, before dinner, he told himself as he swung his legs out from under the sheets, off the mattress and headed for the bathroom.

They were finally going to eat at the restaurant in the Oyster. He had heard many good reviews and was looking forward to the experience.

Sue stood with her back to the island, a coffee mug cradled in her hands, looking out the window where a hummingbird flitted between the lantana and zinnia.

She gave him a smile as he came into the kitchen, squeezed his hand as he leaned over and kissed her, even though he'd kissed her, all of her, not three hours ago. Soon, they'd need to get a full night's sleep.

Not too soon, he hoped.

He kissed her again, then reached for a mug and poured coffee.

"Are you sure you want me to come with you today?"

Rick gripped the coffee carafe a little harder, so he wouldn't splash the hot liquid over the counter or onto his hand.

Carefully, he finished pouring, replaced the carafe, started to answer, then stopped himself.

There was something in Sue's voice he didn't recognize. Rick didn't get a sense of nerves, fear, or reluctance. He'd seen and heard all three many times from Marines under his command.

This was different, and he couldn't place what the something in Sue's voice meant.

Rick chose his words carefully.

"Leave aside that I'd very much like you on the boat today. I understand if you don't want to be so public at the moment about us being together."

Sue's blue eyes sparkled. Her face twisted in humor, and she laughed. The rich, throaty chuckle that Rick loved.

She reached forward, linked her fingers in his.

"Rick. The hospital is a bigger hotbed of gossip than any bar, restaurant, or diner on this island. We're already public."

He thought about the reactions of the nursing staff this past week when he'd visited his mother. The knowing smiles. The glances. The half-heard whispered comments when the nurses thought he wasn't looking or listening.

Sue squeezed his hand. "I don't want you to think you have to take me everywhere with you, or that I'm imposing on something Marine related."

Rick didn't think he'd presented the trip that way. On reflection, he saw how Sue might get that impression.

"I'm going to take a leap of faith that there's something between us that's more than just a few weeks. If I'm right, there will be times when I want to do things without you. Just as I'm sure you'll want to do the same, like gossiping with Beth."

He got a knowing smile and a sparkle of amusement in her green eyes for that.

"I didn't intend to present the expedition in a way that made you feel excluded. It wasn't how we thought of a day sailing. I'd like you to come, and if it helps, Denson's niece, Amy, might appreciate some female company."

He saw something inside her change. Her shoulders relaxed. She leaned into him, her scent clouding his senses in the best way possible.

"I like the more than a few weeks thought," she said. "Count me in. Did you think of drinks and snacks while we're out there?"

Typical mother, Rick thought.

"Provisions are my job," he said. "We'll stop at the store on the way."

Andrew had created a harness that went round Denson's waist and thighs, and under his arms. The harness connected to a line that ran from the end of the boom up to the mast-head and back down to a winch.

"I must be crazy to agree to this," Denson said as the line came tight and he found himself a foot above the seat of his wheelchair.

He continued grumbling as he got higher, but Rick saw the sparkle of fun in the man's eyes and heard the undercurrent of excitement in the veteran's complaints.

When Denson was settled, Rick helped Amy and Sue aboard through the aft swim step. He untied the lines and settled himself in the cockpit as Andrew carefully and skillfully took them out of the marina.

They were maybe a half mile offshore when Andrew eased the engine revolutions back so the boat slowed until it was holding station.

"Sails, Colonel?" Andrew asked Rick.

Rick looked at him, raised an eyebrow. "You have the helm. You're the skipper. Are we putting the sails up?"

Andrew looked stunned for a moment. Rick could almost see the thoughts chasing through his mind, and across his face. Then he grinned.

"Yes, we are," he said, and glanced up at the wind gauge on the top of the mast.

"Turning into the wind," Andrew said. He gave the engine a burst of power and turned the wheel slowly to port.

As the Beneteau swung, Rick put his foot on the seat, gripped the support stanchion for the bimini, ducked his head, and stepped out of the cockpit. The swell was slight, and he made it to the mast without having to reach for a steadying handhold.

Rick slipped the main halyard off the cleat, gave it a tug to make sure it ran clear, and was rewarded by the rustle of canvas as the top of the mainsail lifted slightly.

He looked back toward the cockpit. Denson sat hunched forward, his shoulders tight, giving brief nods as his niece patted his shoulder. Beth sat on the stern seat, on Andrew's right as Rick looked back toward the stern. Her cheeks were a little flushed, but she looked relaxed, the wind ruffling her strawberry blonde hair, her emerald eyes sparkling.

The swinging motion eased to a halt with the bow pointing almost due south. The engine note reduced to a throaty burble as Andrew eased the revolutions back until they were stationary.

"Raise the main when you're ready," Andrew said.

"Raising the main," Rick said.

He caught a whiff of diesel fumes as the wind eddied, blowing the exhaust back at them.

Rick braced himself and pulled the line down toward him. The top of the mainsail shivered, shuddered, and lifted a few feet.

Rick pulled on the line again. He used long sweeping strokes, changing the lead hand with each pull so the sail lifted in stuttering jerky motions. The last few feet took extra effort, and Rick recalled blustery wet days when he was sure he'd be pitched overboard before the sail reached the top of the mast.

One last heave, and he glanced back toward Andrew, who'd been watching the progress.

"You're good," Andrew said.

Rick tied off the halyard, coiled the line, and looked up at the broad expanse of canvas. The sail looked faded, discolored, and worn.

Something else to add to his checklist before Mama came home, he thought as he made his way back to the cockpit.

"Destin or Panama City?" Andrew asked.

Rick saw the young man's face was already turning red in the hot bright sun. He looked over at Denson.

"Your call, Gunny, after Andrew gets some sunscreen."

"Knew I'd forgotten something," Andrew said, and reached into the locker behind the wheel.

As Andrew slathered sunscreen onto his face and arm, Denson said. "Panama City. I see Destin too often. The change of scenery will be good."

Rick made his way aft. On the way, he grabbed a winch handle and unhooked the jib line. He wound the line around the winch, inserted the handle and began turning as Andrew eased the Beneteau to port.

The wind caught the sails. The jib sail unfurled with a

rush and a whoosh and a crack that brought Denson's head up like a hunting dog scenting prey. Beside him, Amy's eyes went wide as the boat tilted. Her hand gripped Denson's upper arm as Rick wound the winch faster, pulling the line taut.

"You're good," Andrew said again. "Let's see how she behaves."

Rick stowed the winch handle and dropped back onto the seat. Sue slid around from the stern to sit beside him. He was surprised when she rested her forearm on his thigh.

Her voice was low. "How does it feel not to be in charge?"

"Unsettling," he said without having to give his answer any real consideration.

She laughed, and he couldn't help himself; he laughed with her.

An hour later, Rick remembered the problem he'd always had with sailing out of Diamond Beach. There really wasn't anywhere to go. None of the restaurants in Destin had dock access. Panama City, where they were headed, was the same.

It wasn't like the Caribbean, or Chesapeake Bay, or even San Francisco Bay where you could sail for a couple of hours, dock at a restaurant for lunch and then sail on.

Or sail from destination to destination like he'd once planned.

"You're deep in thought," Sue said.

Rick came back to himself, checked the set of the sails, saw they were fine, and that Andrew, Amy, and Denson were deep in discussion about how to improve the rope and pulley apparatus they'd used to get Denson on board.

"Thinking about the plans I once had for this boat," he said.

"Circumnavigation?"

"Not quite. Before I joined the Marines, I had this idea to

sail her down to Key West, then all the way north to Bar Harbor."

"Did you tell your parents?"

He smiled at the memory of that conversation. "It was just before Dad got sick. He called it Rick's East Coast Cruise and told me to be careful about picking crew. Mama flat out said I was crazy."

"I think I'd have told Emily the same," Sue said. "Is it still a goal?"

Was it?

He'd thought about it occasionally over the years. Part of him wanted to say it was the dream of a teenager that didn't suit a man in his fifties. Part of him was nervous and excited, the way he always felt when he had a new project, posting, or operation.

Even Israel had been that way at first.

"It may be out of my hands. My situation with the Corps is indeterminate at the moment. I promise I'll tell you everything tonight. In the meantime, I have some ideas for feeding the troops without fighting our way into Panama City."

NINETEEN

*I*ndeterminate.

What the heck did that mean?

Sue played the word through her head on a repeat cycle as she worked in the galley with Amy to unpack the spreads, salsas, and dips she and Rick had selected for lunch.

It was a strange, yet familiar feeling being down here in the galley putting snack together.

She had been on the boat many times in her teenage years. There had always been Rick and Beth and the rest of their friends. It had been crowded, noisy, and fun.

Rick and Andrew had anchored them over a shallow sandbar, Sue remembered from those years. It was warm, airless, and stuffy in the cabin. No breeze flowed through the open hatches.

"Go sit in the fresh air," Sue said to Amy, who moments after coming below had turned pale, with perspiration beading her forehead as she kept swallowing hard.

Amy mumbled thanks and scampered up the companionway.

A good thing it's calm today, Sue thought as she poured

chips and tortilla chips into bowls, her action automatic as she looked round the cabin.

There was a bench seat with cream cushions on the port side, just forward of where she worked. A U-shaped seat opposite with a table, two cabins behind her, the main cabin all the way forward. And a damp, musty smell everywhere.

The seat cushions looked faded and worn with a small nicks and tears that revealed crumbling yellow foam beneath. The varnished woodwork looked scratched and tired.

Everything needed a complete overhaul and airing before Rick took the boat on his east coast cruise.

Sue felt a twist of apprehension in her stomach at the thought. It was only a week, but she'd gotten used to having him in her bed, drinking coffee with him in the morning, sharing frustrations and highlights of her day in the evening.

She didn't want it to end. She worried that indeterminate might mean just that.

Sue pushed the thought away as she picked up the bowls of chips. She couldn't change it and she'd learn tonight exactly what he meant by indeterminate.

At the bottom of the companionway, the Beneteau rocked in the slight swell.

Sue did a quick two-step shuffle, rebalanced herself, then came up the companionway in a rush, a big self-satisfied smile on her face. She might not be able to ride a bike, but she sure as heck hadn't forgotten how to move on a rocking boat.

Rick was watching her. There was a look on his face she couldn't decipher; like he was considering something and hadn't quite reached a decision.

As she placed the bowls on the cockpit table, he came to his feet.

"I'll get the rest," he said.

He squeezed past her, let his fingers trail along her waist and across the small of her back, made her shiver, and she was sure he laughed as he clattered down the steps.

After lunch, the wind had dropped to little more than gusts and eddies that barely filled the sails. The boat rocked, pitched, and swayed for another fifteen minutes before Andrew noticed the distress and discomfort Amy was trying to hide.

"We're going to drop the sails and motor home, so Amy keeps her lunch," Andrew said.

"Copy that," Rick said, then to Sue. "There's Dramamine in the first aid kit under the nav station. I checked and updated everything yesterday."

He stepped out of the cockpit and up to the mast, while Sue dropped into the cabin for the first aid kit. She found the Dramamine and frowned at how basic the kit appeared to be.

Sue shook her head, then again when she saw how clouded the plastic was on the navigation station gauges and readouts.

More things to fix.

Sue suspected it was more the stable ride and the attention from Andrew than the Dramamine that cured Amy, and she was almost back to herself when the Beneteau slid into the slip.

David, who was walking the dock, helped them tie off, and watched as Rick and Andrew used the harness in reverse fashion to get Denton off the boat and into his wheelchair.

Rick helped her down onto the dock, his hand warm in hers.

"Do we need to change for dinner?"

She shook her head. "They're pretty relaxed at this time of year. We can sit either on the terrace or at the bar."

"Sounds good," he said, then frowned as his phone buzzed.

Sue watched as he pulled the phone from his shorts pocket. He glanced at the caller ID and frowned again.

"I have to take this," he said, and answered with. "Hi Alex. What's new?"

He turned away and walked slowly to the end of the dock, intent on what he was being told.

Sue hoped he was getting good news, and watched Amy walk alongside Denson's wheelchair, chatting away to him, bringing a chuckle to the veteran's response.

On the dock beside her, David and Andrew were coiling lines, and folding the harness used to get Denson on and off the boat.

"I've never seen a contraption like that," David said as he handed the harness to Andrew.

Sue saw the flush creep up Andrew's cheeks. Shaved, his hair trimmed close to his skull, clean khaki shorts and a blue polo shirt, Andrew looked nothing like the tortured semi-derelict who'd often frequented her Emergency Room.

"We learned how to improvise."

Even his voice sounded fresh, Sue thought.

David must have had the same reaction.

He said. "We can use that initiative in the yard. We can talk about it over a cold beer, if you're interested. Actually, I'll buy you a beer even if you're not interested."

"I am interested in the yard, and the beer," Andrew said. Then his voice became lower, hesitant, and more serious.

"This has been a good day, but I have bad ones as well."

"We'll work it out," David said. He looked over at Sue. "You joining us?"

She considered declining, then realized she didn't know how long Rick's call would take. She'd also see him from the bar.

"Sounds good," she said.

They were half way along the dock when her own phone

buzzed. For a moment, she considered ignoring it but it was her on call weekend, and she had to be available if there was an emergency or some other crisis at the Medical Center.

She recognized the number, felt her stomach twist, her heart lurch. The warm, bright goodness of the day washed away.

"I'll catch up," Sue said to David as she answered the call.

"What is it, Sarah?"

As bad as she feared.

Rick was still on the phone. He seemed to listen more than talk. He sensed her presence when she was still four or five paces away. He turned to look at her.

His face looked relaxed, she thought. The shadows that had haunted him since she'd seen him that first Friday night at the Medical Center were gone.

She hated to bring them back.

"We need to leave," Sue said. "It's your mom."

TWENTY

*R*ick strode through the lobby of the emergency room. His deck shoes squeaked on the tile floor, making the waiting patients turn their heads and look.

There were only five people in the waiting area. Two groups scattered across the neatly arranged blue plastic chairs, watching the end of a ballgame on the televisions mounted high on the wall out of arm's reach.

It was quiet time on a Saturday afternoon.

There were no outpatients lined up waiting for transport. It was too early for careless husbands to carve their hands open while wrestling with overcooked meat. And much too early for the drunks and other revelers who went a step too far.

Rick was aware of Sue beside him, her stride matching his, her strawberry blonde hair flowing, and no sign of struggle or stress in keeping up with him.

As they reached the reception, Rick recognized the woman from his first visit, searched his memory for her name.

Sue took two long strides, stepped slightly in front of him.

"Hi Tracie," she said. "ICU called about Frances Miller. I'm taking her son up now."

Rick heard something new in Sue's tone. The professional was there, but there was more. Something harsh, clipped, and no-nonsense, like she was walking a fine line of control.

Tracie looked up from the computer screen, her brown eyes wide with surprise. She'd heard it or sensed it as well.

"Oh. Yes. Fine. Want me to call ahead?" Tracie said.

"Good idea," Sue said, then turned to Rick.

She offered a smile that didn't reach her eyes and had no humor. "We'll take the elevator. I don't think I can manage the stairs this time."

The medical team was still in his mother's room when Rick and Sue reached the ICU floor at the Medical Center. He recognized Sarah, the Bahamian nurse. She gave him a smile of recognition, but her face had that closed, professional look he'd seen too many times in the past year.

"I'll get some coffee and cancel our dinner reservation." Sue said.

She touched his arm, squeezed his hand, then hurried back to the elevator.

Rick offered a prayer of gratitude. He'd completely forgotten about their dinner date.

She was going to her office, Rick guessed. Going to brew some of the really good coffee he was learning to appreciate.

He doubted he'd appreciate the quality tonight.

Rick walked down the hallway. It was wide enough for six or seven people to walk abreast, but it felt cramped, closed in and oppressive to him. The lemon scent of the disinfectant and cleaner felt sickening and nauseating rather than fresh and clean.

The door to his mother's room was closed, the blinds

across the window angled so he couldn't see inside. He heard movement and voices in the room. The voices were too low to make out any words.

Rick paced back and forth for a few laps, then dropped into one of the hard, uncomfortable blue plastic chairs that lined the hallway.

The chair reminded him of briefing rooms in bases across the world. Deliberately designed not to be ergonomic, the chair scraped, poked, and stabbed at his legs and back every time he moved.

Intended to keep you awake and alert, Alex had said after one interminable session in Tel Aviv. Rick had agreed with him then, and still did.

Rick let his thoughts return to the call from Alex.

He leaned back, ignoring the twist of plastic that jabbed under his ribs.

Nothing to worry about, Alex had said. It's all sorted.

Easy for Alex to say. It wasn't his career, competence, or mental stability under the microscope.

Rick still hadn't found the right time to tell Sue. Sorted could mean anything, including Leavenworth. Even without the military prison in Kansas, Rick was certain there were caveats, rules, or conditions Alex hadn't had time to explain.

Rick was still picking apart Alex's words in his mind, and trying to find a comfortable position in the chair, when Sue returned with the coffee. She handed him a protein bar as well, then gave a soft smile when Rick glanced at the wall sign prohibiting food in large black lettering.

"My hospital. My rules," she said, then nodded toward the closed door.

"Any news?"

Rick shook his head, crushed the wrapper of the protein bar into his pocket, sipped at the coffee, and took a mouthful of the protein bar. He expected it to be dry, dusty and without flavor, like the bars they carried into action.

It tasted better than he had expected. There was a burst of flavor from something fruity, probably cherry, the slightly bitter bite of dark chocolate and an explosion of sweetness. Honey.

He finished the bar in three bites.

"I'll take no news as a good sign," he said.

They sat together in companionable silence, neither feeling they had to say anything.

When the door to his mother's room opened, the cardiologist, Smith, came out first. His white coat was crumpled, his narrow face almost shrunken in on itself. He looked even shorter than he had when Rick spoke with him before and after the operation.

His team filed out behind him, looking tired and somber. Smith said a few words to each of them, then turned toward Rick and Sue.

He gave Sue a quick nod of recognition, then focused his attention on Rick.

"How is she?" Rick asked.

"Your mother is gravely ill, Mister Miller. It's a testament to her will and determination that she survived this second heart attack. If she gets through the night, she has a chance."

About what Rick had suspected. Actually a little better.

"Can I stay with her?"

"Check at the nurses' station. I doubt they'll have an issue." Then Smith allowed a smile to animate his features and smooth away most of the fatigue.

"If there is a problem, it seems you have an inside track with the management."

Sarah assured Rick there would be no problem.

"We'll be in to check on your mama every hour or so, and we'll bring you water or coffee or whatever you want. The coffee won't be as fancy as Miss Sue's, but it's hot and drinkable."

As Rick turned away from the nurses station, Sue touched his arm.

"Call me when you leave here."

He started to protest. Sue shook her head, lifted her left hand and placed a finger on his mouth. Her voice was soft, serious, and tinged with pain.

"This is something you need to do for yourself."

Her voice faltered then. Rick saw the sheen of tears in her green eyes. She leaned into him then, resting her head on his chest. Her voice was low, her speech slow, like she needed to talk that way to stop the emotion choking her.

"Truth is, I don't know if I can sit beside a hospital bed again and make small talk I don't know is being heard."

It was the first reference she'd ever made to the pain and anguish she'd suffered when her husband was sick.

Rick had never lost a spouse, but he'd sat with the mortally wounded at the hospital in Hadassah and other places.

He understood.

He caught her left hand in his, lifted it to his mouth, kissed her palm and then pulled her into an embrace.

"I understand perhaps better than you know. I'll call you."

He kissed her hard on the mouth, not caring about the audience, squeezed her hard against him and watched until she stepped into the elevator.

Rick sat with Frances in the darkened room. The machines hummed and beeped around him. The only sign his mother was still alive was the slow-moving green line and the digital readouts that monitored her heartbeat, pulse and respiration.

Rick kept her left hand cradled in his and talked.

He told her about the deployment orders to Israel, the

chartered jets that flew his men into Ben Gurion International Airport southeast of Tel Aviv. He told her about his experiences, told her things he'd never told the psychologist, the inquiry, or any other person.

The nurses brought him coffee, and he told Frances about Sue. How he hoped their relationship might develop and grow into something permanent.

And when he ran out of words, he sat there listening to the beep of the monitor and held her hand until she passed.

TWENTY ONE

On Monday, Sue took a personal day. She doubted anyone at the hospital would be surprised.

Rick had slept restlessly, tossing, turning, and thrashing and cursing as a nightmare controlled him.

He was tired, with bags under his eyes, when he kissed her and left for the funeral home.

The house seemed empty without his presence, and that was a surprise. Sue hadn't realized how much Rick had become a part of her everyday life.

She sat on a stool at the kitchen island sipping at her coffee, still felt the warmth of his farewell kiss on her mouth

She allowed herself a smile, glimpsed her reflection in the kitchen window above the sink. Not bad for an older woman who had believed sex was a thing of her past.

Sue thought of Beth, and her smile became broader. Then she thought of her daughter and reached for her phone.

Emily answered on the second ring. "Hi Mom. What are you up to?"

There was a false cheeriness in Emily's voice that made Sue's Mother Alarm chime.

"Are you okay, Emily?"

"I'm always good. The story I'm working on is outside my usual comfort zone, and it's pretty intense."

There was silence for several beats. Sue could almost see her daughter shaking herself, her shoulder-length auburn hair bouncing in time with the movement.

When Emily spoke again, her voice was brighter, more cheerful, and infused with her usual energy.

"You didn't call to hear me whine. What's your news, Mom?"

Better, but Sue still didn't quite believe her.

Suddenly nervous, Sue took a swallow of coffee and a long breath.

"I wanted you to know I'm seeing someone."

"That's wonderful." This time the energy and enthusiasm in Emily's voice were genuine.

"Does he live in Diamond Beach? How did you meet? Do I know him?"

Sue laughed. "Let me catch my breath first."

She took a sip of coffee. It was lukewarm now. She pushed the mug away.

"No, you don't know him. We knew each other in high school. He came back into town when his mother was taken ill, and we reconnected."

"How is his mother?"

"She passed away on Saturday evening."

There was a long pause. "I'm sorry, Mom. It must be hard for you as well. Is he with you? I'd like to offer my condolences properly."

"He left the house earlier to make funeral arrangements."

The words came out before Sue could edit them. She closed her eyes, felt the heat flare on her cheeks.

"So you're really calling to warn me so I don't bounce

through the door unexpectedly one evening and find you two doing the wild thing in the kitchen."

"Emily!" Sue felt her cheeks burn again.

Her daughter laughed long and loud and from deep in her belly. She had inherited Ben's laugh.

"I'm glad, Mom. It's about time. And wherever he is, I know Dad is happy too. He wouldn't like how you've shut yourself away like a hermit these past few years."

There was a noise in the background, and before Sue could argue with Emily's comment, her daughter said.

"Got someone at the door. I look forward to meeting him. What's his name? Love you. Bye."

"Rick," Sue said, but she was talking to a dead line.

TWENTY TWO

$\mathcal{I}$t took a week to organize the funeral.

Once the documents, certificates, and affidavits were in place, Rick agreed on a date with the funeral home, and then the uncles and their families descended on Diamond Beach.

The last notes of the processional hymn faded away. There was a rustling of movement behind Rick as everyone sat down.

He was still stunned at how many people were in the chapel to say farewell to his mother. He knew she'd known many people. She was a person who never knew a stranger. Rick guessed he took after his father in that respect.

As everyone settled, the minister, Meg, if he recalled her name correctly, looked at him, gave a soft smile and indicated the lectern.

Rick pushed to his feet. The dark charcoal suit jacket was tight across his shoulders, loose around his legs like baggy sweatpants, and barely comfortable around his waist.

Sue had suggested he wear his uniform.

He had been firm about the no.

Today was about his mother, not her son parading in a uniform with medals and honors he might not have the right to wear when the results of the inquiry were announced.

Alex was confident Rick would be cleared.

Rick wasn't so sure. He'd sat on more inquiries and courts martial than he cared to remember.

The facts weren't always the determining factor. In this inquiry, politics was a serious consideration. Maybe the most important. It was what the Pentagon and probably the White House wanted that would determine his fate.

He ran a hand through the stubble on his scalp, stood for a moment, then walked the half-dozen steps to the lectern.

It felt like the long march along the polished wood floors at Quantico when he testified to the Inquiry.

Meg gave him a sympathetic smile as he reached the lectern and stepped to one side.

When he'd followed the coffin into the chapel, Rick had been aware there were many people there. Only now, looking down the chapel toward the front entrance, did Rick appreciate just how many people were here.

Sue, of course. Mark Wilson with his wife. Beth and her husband Michael. Andrew sat with his head down, fingers twisting and untwisting.

A lot of people. Even Sheriff Carter, who stood at the back of the chapel with his partner, whose name Rick had never learned.

He sensed the anticipation and interest in the congregation. They knew he'd left town at eighteen, joined the service, and returned occasionally.

There were many sheets of paper crumpled on Sue's kitchen floor from where Rick had tried to put the right words together for this moment.

None of those words worked, and he realized they

weren't supposed to. The only option was to go back to the beginning.

Rick cleared his throat and said.

"One thing about growing up in somewhere like Diamond Beach is you know everyone. That can be very good and really bad. Mama knew everyone, especially my teachers. She always knew when I had school work I was trying to avoid."

There was a ripple of amusement through the congregation. He'd touched on something they could relate to.

Rick felt himself relax a little.

"There are people I've met in the past few days I immediately remember. Others I recall but can't place a name, and there are some who I see here this morning, of whom I have no recollection. To you especially, I apologize. You're all here today because of the impact my mother, Frances, had on your lives. Sons, probably more than daughters, never appreciate that impact until it's too late."

Rick paused when he felt his throat tighten. He'd sworn he wouldn't come apart during the service but it was harder than he expected.

He swallowed, gripped the hard wooden edge of the lectern, felt the wooden edges bite into his palms, grounding him in the present.

Rick took a breath and continued.

"When I left Diamond Beach, I knew inside that Mama wasn't happy. She wanted me to be an accountant like my father and my uncles." He nodded his head toward the two elderly gentlemen in suits and ties sat in the front row.

"Less than happy," Uncle Paul grumbled, and there was another wave of amusement.

Rick caught Sue's eye. She smiled, green eyes sparkling. She nodded encouragement.

"I didn't come back and see my mother often enough, so I

didn't know she was still sailing the boat I grew up with. I didn't know how she helped people like Andrew. And I never appreciated the insight she had about some feelings I had all those years ago."

He had to pause then to wipe away the tears that blurred his vision.

"Someone recently reminded me that mothers have special powers. It's part of who they are."

Rick tilted his head up toward the varnished beams of loblolly pine that supported the ceiling, although his eyes looked much higher.

"I'm sure she's looking down now, chuckling to herself that it took me so long to work out many things," he put his right hand over his heart. "I'll try, Mama. I'll try."

Fortunately, it was only a few steps back to his seat, and there was nothing to get in his way.

As Rick sat down, Uncle Paul reached over, squeezed his hand.

"Your mother was the best," Paul said, then carefully pushed to his feet and moved with slow, arthritic steps to the lectern.

"Frances was so much more than my brother's wife. She was a mother, sister, and friend to her husband Peter, Henry here," he gestured at his brother sitting in the front row alongside Rick. "And myself."

Rick heard the words, but they were like a bee droning through flowers as it searched for pollen.

The rest of the service was a hazy blur, and afterward as everyone filed out of the chapel, he shook hands, hugged most everyone, and heard again and again what a wonderful person his mother had been.

Sentiments he knew himself, and had finally told her many times in those last hours by her bedside.

Rick planned a short reception at his mother's house. Sodas, wine, and simple finger foods.

When he stepped into the house, he saw Uncle Paul with a plastic plate and a pile of pasta he attacked with a fork. The rich flavors of the sauce, the meat, and the nutty crust of parmesan lifted into the surrounding air, smelled, tasted and felt familiar. The sensations tweaked his appetite like nothing had done since his mother died.

He turned to Sue who stood beside him, the way she'd done constantly through these last days.

"Is that what I think it is?"

"Yes it is," Beth said, coming up behind him and wrapping her arms around his waist.

Rick turned, folded her into his arms. "Your Mom guarded that lasagna recipe like it was all the gold in Fort Knox."

"It took me ten years to get it from her, and then lots of practice," Beth said with a laugh. "It's just about the only thing Sue will eat at my house if Michael isn't grilling or smoking something."

"That's not exactly true," Sue said. "Sometimes I bring pizza."

Beth slid out of Rick's arms, clutched her hand to her chest just above her heart. "Be careful of her, Rick. She can kill with one sentence."

There was a tease in her voice, and merriment in her eyes. His mood lifted, although Beth's words echoed in his head.

It was exactly what Sue had done to him all those years ago.

He caught the scent of the lasagna again and let the dark thoughts slide away. It was in the past. He and Sue were good. Today was about Mama, not his demons.

Rick slid out of his suit jacket, tugged his black tie off, and dropped them both on a chair as he headed into the kitchen for the lasagna.

The lure of the lasagna kept people longer than they intended, but within two hours everyone except Sue had left.

Sue tossed the last of the paper and plastic plates, cups and cutlery into a black contractor bag, then reached into a cupboard, pulled out a bottle of wine and poured two glasses.

"Beth left us this and another lasagna at my house," Sue said.

Rick took the glass, then put it on the island as he heard someone come in through the front door.

"Mom?"

Sue looked unconcerned, pleased almost, but maybe a little nervous.

"In the kitchen," Sue said. "On your right."

A young woman appeared. Rick placed her at about five three or five four, close to Sue's height. She wore a black knee-length skirt, black shell top, and a black blazer. Long auburn hair cascaded in a waterfall over her shoulder. Her eyes were as blue as Sue's were green.

"I'm sorry I'm late," she said. "The traffic on ten was bumper to bumper."

Then she saw Rick, or became aware he was there. There was a flare of recognition in her eyes. Her smooth face twisted into a frown, the look in her eyes as hard as the sapphires they favored.

Her voice was cold, harsh and bitter.

"I don't know why you're here Colonel Miller. I thought you were in custody where you belong, but I'd like you to move away from my mother. We don't want any more unexplained deaths, do we?"

"Emily! What are you saying? Rick?"

Clearly sentences as weapons ran in the family.

Rick closed his eyes. Part of him really wanted the wine

by his left hand but he knew it would taste like vinegar. At least Mama wouldn't have to suffer the humiliation of the pointing and whispering and innuendo.

"Aren't you going to say anything, Rick?"

There was pain in Sue's voice.

How much could he say that wouldn't rip up the papers he'd signed and give the Board of Inquiry all they needed to proceed with the Court Martial some of them were desperate for?

He'd wanted to tell Sue differently. A way for her to understand the decisions he had to make in a split second. No time to analyze, or plan, or consider. Just act.

"The Pentagon convened an Inquiry to determine if I should be Court Martialed for the death of five Marines in a barrack room in Hebron."

"You killed them?"

He really thought Sue might have understood. She met with and spoke to veterans all day. Men like Denson and Andrew. Unless she was so far removed from reality in her office.

Rick looked at the two women. He guessed Emily took after her father, but right now they were united. Both had their arms crossed, shutting him out, their eyes hard, expressions cold.

Rejection.

"I'll let you have your reunion," he said, grateful his voice didn't betray the anguish and desolation that ripped through his body.

"Close up the house when you're done. I'll finish everything later."

Neither of them tried to stop him, which he supposed was a good thing. The afternoon air on the porch was as hot, humid, and confining as it had felt in the house.

Rick weaved round his rental car the blue SUV he assumed was Emily's.

He needed activity, action, or movement, and set off along the street at a fast march with no actual idea where he was going.

TWENTY THREE

he rack of the slamming front door snapped Sue out of the endless whirl of thoughts spinning through her head.

She wasn't sure how she felt

"He said his situation was indeterminate," she said, recalling Rick's words on the Beneteau.

"He didn't elaborate?"

Sue shook her head. "There were a lot of other people about. We had dinner planned at the Oyster that evening and he promised to tell me everything."

"Why didn't he?" Emily's voice was softer now,

"His mother died."

Emily winced. "And then I walked and gave him both barrels.

Sue reached for the glass Rick had left behind. She prayed there wasn't any of his taste or scent on the glass.

Sue had seen the devastation on his face as he left, although he'd tried hard to mask it. Recognized it because it matched her own feelings.

The wine tasted sharp, sour, and bitter. She made a face,

put the glass away and turned back to find Emily's arms around her.

"I'm sorry, Mom. I was so surprised to see him, I spoke without thinking. You really care about him don't you."

"I love him," Sue said, and was grateful Beth wasn't there to hear it and crow about catching up.

"Then we'll fix it," Emily said.

Sue was about to say that was unlikely when a musical tone cut through the silence.

Ride of the Valkyries.

Sue slid out from Emily's arms, crossed the living room and felt through the pockets of the jacket Rick had left behind. She fumbled with the phone, twisting and turning it, praying she'd get to the slider before the call went to voicemail.

"Rick. It's Alex. I'm sorry to interrupt during your Mama's funeral but this is important, and you need to hear it."

Sue took a long breath, realized her hands were trembling and gripped the phone a little tighter.

"I'm sorry, Rick isn't here at the moment. I'm Susan Williams. A friend."

Oh Lord how it hurt to say that.

"Sue? The Sue he was telling me about last week? You've got yourself a good man there. You should hold onto him, although I don't think he plans to let you go."

Tears flooded into her eyes at his words. She tried to talk without her voice cracking, knew she failed.

"He may be rethinking that. There were some things said when he met my daughter Emily that may be irrevocable."

The last thing she expected was a peal of laughter.

"Let me guess," Alex said between more laughs at his end. "He's been his typical say nothing, stoic self. Someone learned something, added two and two, made five, and instead of a full explanation, Rick let himself be run off."

"Pretty much, except it was my daughter and I that ran him off."

"Ouch."

"That covers it," and then she had a thought. "Alex, If I put you on speaker so Emily can hear, are you able to tell us what the media can't or won't? What really happened."

For a moment, she thought he was going to say no, then he said.

"No reason not to. It will all be public tomorrow."

Sue pushed Rick's jacket to one side and sat in the chair. Emily perched on the arm, her arm around Sue's shoulders.

"We had just finished a five-day patrol down to Galilee and got back to the barracks in Hebron," Alex began. "Colonels aren't supposed to be at the sharp end like that, but Rick was never good at following those sorts of orders."

"Was he hurt?" Sue couldn't stop herself.

"Not this time."

Sue thought she caught amusement in his voice at her question.

"We had some casualties, though. We'd just finished the debrief when Rick said there was something wrong. Something badly wrong. He has a sense for that. It's scary because he's always right.

"When we got to the barrack room, two Marines were shooting at the others. There were six or seven men down. Rick took about half a second to assess the situation and shot them both."

"What caused the two men to behave like that? A breakdown?" Emily asked.

Alex's laugh this time was a harsh bark, short, and without humor.

"That's probably what the official report will say. Reality is they were deep-cover radicals who'd been in the Marines for ten years. One of them had a Silver Star for bravery.

"I don't know why they acted when they did, but Rick saved a lot of lives that afternoon. We found half a dozen fragmentation grenades on their bodies."

Sue wasn't sure if she was more afraid of the next question or the answer. She asked anyway.

"Will he face a court martial?"

"No. The Pentagon and the White House really want to keep this quiet. Your breakdown theory will probably become reality. Rick will fade quietly into the sunset."

"When you see him, tell him that, and tell him he's an idiot. I'll be there in the next day or two. I'm looking forward to meeting you, Sue. And you, Emily."

The line went dead. Sue looked away from the phone to Emily. There were tears in her daughter's eyes, and she felt the sting in her own eyes.

"I'm sorry, Mom. All the reports and all my sources agreed. I never thought to question it."

"You're writing a story about Rick?"

The words came out sharper than Sue intended. Or maybe they didn't.

"No." Emily slid off the arm of the chair. "I'm writing a story about something else, and there were links and threads that connected to your Rick. That's how I recognized him so easily."

Sue released a sigh that was a huff. "I'm not sure he's my Rick anymore."

"You're just going to let him go. Come on, Mom, what about the young nurse who sidetracked Janice Wesley so she got alone time with handsome Doctor Ben?"

"He told you about that?"

Emily smiled. The first time that afternoon.

"Daddy first told me that story when I was twelve or thirteen. I heard it again many times toward the end when it was really the painkillers talking."

Emily reached down, grabbed Sue's hands and pulled her to her feet.

"Do you have any idea where Rick might have gone?"

Sue shook her head, then realized maybe she did know.

Hope blossomed inside her, light, bright and energizing like dawn after a long night.

"Maybe I do, but we have to go home first."

TWENTY FOUR

There was a strong breeze coming off the gulf, bringing with it the smell of salt, seaweed, and ozone.

Rick marched toward it like he was moving from one end of a battlefield to the other. Military forced march. He was vaguely aware of other people passing him, or being passed. He'd been back in Diamond Beach long enough that some folks recognized him again and called out greetings or expressed condolences about his mother.

Rick nodded, smiled, and made all the right responses. No need for them to think he was a complete jerk.

Rick came to a halt where the road ended at the railing above the seawall. The marina was off to his right. Gulls wheeled and cried, diving into the water for pieces of trash they thought were food. Halyards slapped against masts in the marina. He looked over, fancied he saw the Beneteau, knew it was probably wishful thinking, but it gave him an idea and a purpose.

Someone had left the dock gate propped open. Rick was

grateful for the oversight, as the keys were in his jacket back at Mama's house.

He slipped his shoes and socks off before going aboard. Thankfully, there was no sign of Andrew. He wasn't in the mood for conversation of any kind with anyone.

Might not be for a while.

He'd leave everything at Sue's. He couldn't bring himself to face her again. Not with that look of horror and condemnation in her eyes.

The lawyers could handle the sale of Mama's house and wire the money to wherever he ended up.

He'd take the boat east, he decided. A quick run to Panama City to shake out the kinks, relearn how to sail solo, and replace essentials. Then down to Tampa and on to Key West.

In Key West, he could try to drink away the cold, hard knot in his stomach.

Rick laughed at himself then. A short, harsh bark that sounded like the gulls above and carried no humor.

The drink hadn't helped him forget Sue the last time.

He doubted it would work this time.

Rick lifted the wooden panels away from the main hatch, took them below with him and dropped them on the loveseat forward of the galley area. He reached up and unclipped the hatches, pushing them wide open. Air flowed in, rustled the paper chart on the nav station.

The boat smelled musty and felt a little damp. She needed airing out and some love and attention. He made his way forward to the main cabin. There was an unpleasant smell from the bathroom that made his nose wrinkle and his eyes water.

The boat rocked. The fenders rubbed and squeaked against the dock. Rick leaned across the mattress to look through the porthole and didn't see anything except pilings and a boat moored next to him.

Probably wake from something passing in the main channel.

Between the trip with Denson, and today, Rick had a good mental list of everything that needed cleaning, repairing, or replacing, and three levels of priority.

He made his way back through the cabin to the companionway. He'd check the anchor and anchor chain, add those to this list if needed and be out of here in the next hour.

At the top of the companionway, he froze.

Sue sat in the cockpit, pretty much in the same place as when they'd taken Denson out. There were two insulated mugs in her hands. She'd changed into jeans and a pink Diamond Beach sweatshirt. Her face was pale, blonde hair loose and hanging like a waterfall to her shoulders, wisped and frizzed in the humidity. Her eyes were puffy, the green almost white. She looked like she'd been crying.

"I'm hoping we can talk," she said.

There was a hesitancy in her voice, a nervousness like she expected rejection.

Rick thought about it for an instant. Thought about sending her away with harsh, vicious words. Even as the thought came to him, he knew he couldn't do it.

He reached forward, took the mug from her left hand, and tried not to react to the spark when their fingers brushed.

Rick sat on the opposite side of the center console. "I'm listening."

Sue put her mug on the console and reached into her pocket. She pulled out his phone and offered it. This time he managed not to let their hands touch.

"Alex called. I answered and asked some questions. He

says there'll be no court martial." Her look changed then, shifting into a tentative impish grin.

"He also said you're an idiot. He didn't say it, but I am too. I should have let you explain as best you could. Why didn't you tell us?"

Rick caught the aroma of the coffee. Dark roast with a hint of chocolate. His new favorite.

He felt the dark knot inside begin to him ease.

"Alex is right as usual. I was going to tell you before dinner on the night Mama died. After that, everything got out of hand."

He took a sip of the coffee and decided he had nothing left to lose. Not where Sue was concerned.

"I love you, Sue. Did at eighteen and do now. I don't want to come between you and Emily. She's too important."

"You won't. She's waiting for me to give her an all clear so she can come apologize and meet you properly. Before I do that, I have to know how indeterminate your situation is."

"It's very determinate now, if you're okay with having me around," he said, reaching across the console to take her hand.

"Very okay," she said.

She pulled him to his feet so he could kiss her, after which she waved at Emily, then said. "You need some work done in the galley and the nav station, plus new sails before you even consider Rick's East Coast Cruise."

The knot was gone now, unraveled like it had never existed.

Rick tapped the side of his head with his forefinger as he worked his way around the console so he could hold Sue. Really hold her this time.

"I have a list up here," he said. "I might need some help with crew though."

Sue shook her head firmly.

"Crew is sorted," she said. She hooked her arms around his neck, letting him inhale the peach, mango, citrus scent of her.

He leaned down to kiss her as she molded her body against his. Her mouth opened to accept and welcome him.

145

EPILOGUE

ALEXANDER DONOVAN THE FOURTH. Alex, to his friends, stood to one side of the festivities at Diamond Beach Marina. He watched from under a broad-brimmed ball cap as his friend, mentor, and former commanding officer, Rick Miller, hugged a petite blonde to his side.

They weren't married yet, but Alex knew it was just a question of time.

This was his eighth or ninth visit to Diamond Beach, and he had to admit, the island was getting to him, making him miss it every time he left.

He'd met Sue Williams on his first visit as well and liked her. Liked her a lot. She was good for Rick and brought out the best in him.

Alex hadn't seen Rick look so happy and relaxed in years. If ever.

Beyond the patio where their party was located, one boat

stood out in the marina. The Beneteau had been painted, polished, and scrubbed. A new mainsail was flaked along the boom, and a new jib sail wrapped in place around the forestay. Bunting in red, white, and blue hung from the life-lines, the bimini, and dock lines.

Alex estimated it would take most of the next morning to clear the decorations before Rick and Sue could take the boat out to begin their East Coast Cruise. Down to Key West as a first leg, then the long haul up to Bar Harbor in Maine.

He hoped they'd break their journey long enough to stay at his home in Rhode Island for a few days. His family's home really, but his parents were in Europe until Thanksgiving, so at the moment, it was his home.

A flash of auburn hair caught his attention.

Sue's daughter, Emily. Cool, confident, and self-assured. She'd been polite and reserved when they met earlier in the day.

No surprise there. She was a beautiful woman, maybe a year or two younger than him, and obviously skilled at keeping people at arms-length until she knew them better.

Alex understood that. He'd been doing it himself almost since he could walk and talk.

He spotted another loner on the far side of the crowd. Andrew Jenkins. Andrew wore shorts, flip-flops, a Diamond Beach Marina T-shirt, and looked uncomfortable in the crowd.

Rick had told him about Andrew; acombat engineer who'd had a bad time in the Middle East and still suffered. Andrew had found a niche at the Marina and worked hard with Rick refurbishing the Beneteau.

Andrew's restless, Rick had told Alex. I think he needs a new challenge. Let me know if you have any ideas.

Alex had some ideas.

He eased his way around the perimeter toward Andrew. Time to see if the ideas were worth anything.

"Good to see you, Major," Andrew said as Alex reached him.

"It's just Alex now," he said.

He'd put his papers in a month ago. He hadn't told his parents yet, but he knew they'd be relieved.

"You did some great work on the boat," Alex continued. "However, I seem to sense an air of restlessness about you. Am I right?"

Andrew went still. His voice was low, and cautious. Suspicious even.

"Why would you say that?"

Alex laughed softly. No sense in attracting attention to this conversation.

"I was Rick's XO for four years. You learn many things fast with him or you don't survive. How close am I, and what happened to Amy?"

"You're close enough," Andrew admitted. He focused on his beer bottle for a few seconds. His fingers picked at the label, worrying the edge until he peeled strips of paper away.

"Amy has a serious boyfriend at Florida State, so I'm definitely in the friend zone with her. As for what I want, I don't know what I'm looking for. Just that it's something different."

"There's an organization called Engineers Without Borders," Alex said. "Maybe call them and talk to them."

Andrew took a swig of his beer, then another. "I'll maybe do that," he said. Then. "You have incoming, sir. Ten-o'clock."

There was a rustle of movement, and Andrew was gone. Alex looked ahead and to his left, saw Rick and Sue coming toward him. Emily stalked alongside, her posture stiff and unyielding. He guessed she was upset or annoyed about something.

"Need a favor," Rick said as the trio reached him.

"I can get a rideshare," Emily said.

"Not to Pensacola," Sue said.

Alex heard the firm, no-nonsense tone in her voice and suspected the argument between them had been going on for some time.

"Her car won't start, even with a jump," Rick said. "We can't get anyone to look at it until tomorrow, and Emily has interviews first thing."

"I'll be happy to drive you over," he said.

It gave him the opportunity to learn what exactly Emily did for a living that had her, a civilian, recognizing Rick when nothing was released.

And he got to spend several hours with a beautiful woman.

AUTHOR'S NOTE

When I wrote the scene in the emergency room with Rick and Denson, the idea of US troops with boots on the ground in Israel seemed far-fetched and incredibly unlikely.

I spent some time thinking about changing the scenario. The Middle East is an emotive topic at best, and regrettably, an area of ongoing conflict for most of my life - actually for thousands of years if you go back to the Sumerians and Assyrians.

And then there was the 2024 US Presidential election. The suggestion of US soldiers in Gaza, the strikes into Iran by Israel and the US.

Boots on the ground didn't seem so far-fetched after all, so I left it alone.

I do however continue to pray that boots on the ground as mentioned in this story remains where it should be - fiction.

ABOUT THE AUTHOR

International selling author Richard Freeborn writes in many genres from historical and mystery to romance and thrillers.

Currently Richard writes stories in several series including historical mysteries set in Ancient Babylon, the Dune Crest current day mysteries, the time travel Puzzle Store series, and contemporary romances set in Diamond Beach, somewhere along Florida's panhandle.

For more information about Richard's books and projects, please visit his website at https://www.richardfree born.com

You can find Richard's books here: books2read.com/ RichardFreeborn/

THE BODY OF THE SERPENT

ONE

The Citation shuddered and juddered as it ran through a patch of turbulence. Paula's head bounced off the padded headrest. She sat forward, and gave up any pretense of trying to sleep, even though her body cried out for the rest.

Thirty hours ago she'd been ready to finish her day at the tungsten mine in northern Norway when she took the urgent call from the CEO.

After that it was a two bounce trip to Vancouver, a quick briefing, and more bounces across Asia to the islands of Tohay in the Indian Ocean where the company was test dredging for manganese and cobalt on the ocean floor.

Invasion, sabotage, and a volcanic eruption.

The dredging operation was stalled, tying up thousands

of dollars of capital, and the operations manager had disappeared.

Your family is from Tohay. You know the people. Get it fixed, the CEO had said, and teased the prospect of an executive position in Vancouver as a reward for success.

A reward that didn't hold the same attraction it had two or three years ago.

Paula shifted in her seat, checked her watch, which was still on European time. She estimated there was an hour of flight time remaining.

They were in smooth air now, so Paula unbuckled herself, and stood, smiling at the one advantage of being five-feet-three inches. She could stand upright in the Citation's cabin. She pushed her knuckles into the small of her back, trying to knead the kinks out. She felt something click. The dull ache that had plagued her since the refueling stop in Singapore disappeared.

Paula walked the few steps forward to the tiny galley, set the coffee machine to espresso and poured two helpings into the china mug with the blue corporate logo stamped on the side.

Back in her seat, she sipped the hot bitter liquid, and felt the fatigue fade into the background.

Paula opened the blue information folder they'd given her in Vancouver, set it beside the legal pad and her favorite automatic pencil. There wasn't much in the file, and she'd already read it twice. This third time was to decide on her action plan.

In all likelihood the plan would be useless soon after she landed, but at least she'd have something to work with.

The first item was to secure the operations center, and then find the manager. She knew about Roger Davis, and thankfully, had never worked with him. He had a toxic reputation and Paula was never quite sure why he'd been given a second chance. A third one really if the rumors about the Chilean accident were even half true. She made a note to check the accuracy of all the test results, especially the good ones.

When the Citation began its final approach, she had two pages of notes and a solid plan in her head.

When the jet touched down, Paula tilted her head and watched through the tiny window as the pilot taxied up and came to a stop on the left side of the airport buildings.

Or rather, the remains of the airport buildings.

She remembered from her last visit, the Customs Hall was a wood-walled shed with a metal roof. Now there was the burned skeleton of a building with charred wood and twisted metal support beams. A pair of uniformed men stood by the ruins watching the activity beyond the ruined buildings.

Paula look toward where their attention was focused, and saw a drab painted transport airplane with Indian Air Force markings. Teams of uniformed men and women unloaded pallets of supplies.

She pushed the blue folder and her action plan into her laptop bag, collected that and her carryon bag. The pilot, a squat man with a chubby face and sandy hair, had the door open, and steps lowered when she reached the front of the aircraft. He offered to take her bag but she shook her head.

"I'm good," she said. "You leave in the morning?"

He nodded. "There's no fuel to be had here. We have enough to return to Singapore. If you need to evacuate get us a message and we'll collect you."

"If I need to evacuate, the whole team comes," Paula said. "We'll need more than your eight seats."

The pilot nodded again. "Remember it's an option."

Paula took the steps slowly. She breathed the hot humid air carefully, and squinted against the sun's glare. She congratulated herself she'd thought to wear combat boots instead of wedges or heels. The boots looked better with her beige cargo pants and sapphire-blue golf shirt and more practical for the conditions she expected.

At the bottom of the steps, she reached into the side pouch of her carryon, pulled out a ball cap and sunglasses.

She twisted her rust-red hair up under the ball cap and settled the sunglasses in place.

Now that she could see without screwing her eyes almost shut, Paula wiped the sweat off her forehead, and looked around.

The interior of the transport plane was still nearly full of cargo. Paula guessed it would take another three or four hours to finish the unloading. The pallets coming off the transport were stacked away from the aircraft near the remains of the Customs building.

Teams of people pulled the plastic wrapping off the pallets, inspected the boxes and crates. They worked with feverish intensity. Paula heard little conversation as the cargo was separated and loaded onto trucks, and into cars.

None of the vehicles looked newer than five or six years old.

Paula started toward the ruins of the Customs Building, still watching the loading. She was maybe thirty paces from the charred skeleton when one of the loaders stumbled.

He was a big man with a frizz of iron gray hair, a belly rolling down over his belt.

The stack of boxes in his arms toppled to the floor.

His dark face suddenly gray was twisted in pain. His right hand reached for his chest. Paula saw him gasping for breath as his collapsed.

A woman screamed.

Everyone seemed frozen in place.

Paula heard the chatter of insects and trill of the birds.

She released the handle of her carryon, shrugged the backpack off her shoulder and ran.

People crowded round the fallen man when she got there. Paula pushed through the crowd, using her elbows to move forward, ignoring the grumbles and complaints. Just like she had on the rush-hour subway in New York when she did EMT training at the Murray Hill Trauma Center.

A figure was crouched over the fallen man, blocking her way.

"You a doctor?" She asked.

He shifted, turned his head and looked up at her.

Paula had never seen eyes so green, so brilliant. It looked like he could see into her soul and her breath hitched.

He shook his head.

"Get out of the way then."

Paula put her hand on his shoulder to push him aside.

Big mistake.

It was like she'd touched a live power line. The energy and attraction sparked up her arm and into those parts of her body that had lain dormant for so long. Paula hissed a breath, moved her arm and turned away, but not before she'd seen the way his nostrils flared, and his beautiful emerald eyes went wide.

"You want him to have a chance of living, get out of the way."

It was situations like this in mining camps far from civilization that inspired her to get her EMT qualification. At Murray Hill she'd do a full evaluation. Here, like every other occasion in the field, there was no time.

And no time to argue with idiots who didn't know what they were doing.

She slid round him, dropped to her knees, assessing the patient as she did so.

Paula saw the hint of blue on the man's lips, saw the lack

of movement on the man's chest, the sheen of sweat on his lined brow.

She felt for the radial pulse on the right wrist, and twisted her head back to Green Eyes.

"If you really want to help, get me an AED. A defibrillator. There's one on the Citation if the transport isn't equipped."

No pulse. Paula moved her hand, her fingers feeling in the fleshy folds of his neck for the carotid.

Still nothing.

"Starting compressions," she said, like there was a team round her rather than frightened spectators and Green Eyes, although she'd felt him move away and hoped like crazy he was getting her the AED.

She counted to thirty out loud, gave him two hard breaths of mouth to mouth, then started the compressions again.

Paula was halfway through the third cycle of compressions. Her arms ached, sweat dripped into her eyes, and her voice was getting hoarse. She wondered how much longer she could keep this up, when she was aware someone had kneeled down on the opposite side of the patient.

"I'm Elsa. I'm a nurse," the woman said, her voice soft, reassuring, and tinged with a German accent.

"You're doing great. Can you keep going while I set up the defibrillator?"

Paula nodded without breaking her count.

She reached thirty again, gave another set of mouth to mouth and heard the whine as the defibrillator powered up.

"Start again, while I cut his shirt away," Elsa said.

"Got it," Paula said, and started again, confident enough in her rhythm now that she could look up.

Elsa looked to be in her mid to late forties, with close-cropped gray hair a narrow face and intense brown eyes. She wore a long brown dress that looked like a nun's habit. A crucifix hung from a sort chain round her neck. Her hands were steady as she used scissors to slice the left side of the man's t-shirt from hem to neckline.

And an aura of calm that made Paula immediately envious.

Paula's mind came back to the present when Elsa said.

"Stop compression and take that shirt off him."

Paula reached over, grabbed the ragged edges of fabric and drew it toward her, wiping up the sweat on the man's hair covered chest as he did so.

"Good," Elsa said approvingly.

Paula watched as Elsa placed the paddles on the man's chest. The nurse studied the readout for a moment, then in a loud voice said, "Clear!"

The words sounded more like klar to Paula. She shuffled her knees back a few inches.

The charge hit the man's body.

His body jerked. Paula leaned forward ready to restart the compressions when he wheezed. There was a sound like a long moan as he sucked in a long breath and his eyelids fluttered.

Paula helped Elsa roll him into the recovery position.

"I've got him now," Elsa said.

Paula shuffled back, pushed slowly to her feet. She wiped her hands on the shoulders of her golf shirt. The fabric was as damp as her hands. Instead, she used her cargo pants as a towel.

Some of the crowd chattered at her, telling her what a great thing she'd done, patted her on the back, and offered her bottles of water, which she gratefully accepted

When Paula was free of the crowd, and taking long swallows from the lukewarm water, she looked around for Green Eyes. There was no sign of him, and she was surprised at the disappointment that surged through her.

Thieves in the Temple

Jacob fought desperately to save Jerusalem from the Babylonian invaders. Injured and exiled, Jacob builds a new life among his former enemies in the city of Babylon.

As the Babylonians celebrate their New Year, Jacob uncovers a conspiracy threatening the freedom and lives of every Exile.

Uncertain who to trust Jacob unravels the threads of deceit into a compelling climax that saves not just the Exiles, but Jacob himself.

Get Thieves in the Temple, the first Jacob and Miriam mystery at: books2read.com/Thieves

Death at a Wedding

Jacob fought desperately to save Jerusalem from the Babylonian invaders. Injured and exiled, Jacob now builds a new life among his former enemies in the city of Babylon.

An unexpected death makes Jacob reassess everything he believes. Are his friends being truthful. Are the priests honest, or are darker forces at work in Babylon?

Pulling back the layers of lies and half-truths leads Jacob to a shocking last confrontation.

Get Death at a Wedding, the second Jacob and Miriam mystery at: https://books2read.com/DeathataWedding

The Corpse in the Courtyard

Jacob is devastated when he discovers the body of an old friend dumped at his home. The murder drags him into a conspiracy he's tried to avoid for many months. At odds with his own people, and the priests of the Babylonian temple, Jacob must rely on Miriam to determine truths and falsehoods from people neither of them trust.

It takes another violent death to point Jacob and Miriam in the right direction. A direction that threatens to cost Jacob his life, and condemn every Judean Exile into slavery.

Get The Corpse in the Courtyard, the third Jacob and Miriam mystery at: https://books2read.com/TheCorpseInTheCourtyard

Babylon Collections

Beginnings in Babylon

books2read.com/BeginningsInBabylon

Unexpected Companions

books2read.com/u/38yXv7

Making a New Start

books2read.com/NewStart

The Puzzle Store

Tales from the Puzzle Store
books2read.com/Puzzle
Christmas at the Puzzle Store
books2read.com/u/bxa70e

Other Collections

Call Me Rhys

books2read.com/CallMeRhys

The Vatican Shadows

books2read.com/VaticanShadows

Mageweaver

books2read.com/Mageweaver

A Frailty of Heroes

books2read.com/Frailty

A Bag of Bodies

books2read.com/BagOfBodies

The Beach Bar on the Dune

https://books2read.com/u/3GJl0d

From Ceres to Vesta

https://books2read.com/u/brEaeM

Where Infinity Begins

https://books2read.com/u/47091N